CW01276903

The Goat Herder

James Corfe

Copyright © 2025 James Corfe

All rights reserved, including the right to reproduce this book, or portions thereof in any form. No part of this text may be reproduced, transmitted, downloaded, decompiled, reverse engineered, or stored, in any form or introduced into any information storage and retrieval system, in any form or by any means, whether electronic or mechanical without the express written permission of the author.

This is a work of fiction. Names and characters are the product of the author's imagination and any resemblance to actual persons, living or dead, is entirely coincidental.

The views expressed in this work are solely those of the author and do not necessarily reflect the views of the publisher, and the publisher hereby disclaims any responsibility for them.

ISBN: 9798291963975

PublishNation
www.publishnation.co.uk

About the Author

James started out in accountancy, becoming general manager of the trading arm of a public company aged twenty nine. He gave it up three years later to free his mind and his life has since been a series of projects. He taught English language to foreign students over a four year period and has had several small businesses, including more recently woodworking and sculpture in medieval art, which is a passion, as is his music, philosophy and his writing. Described by friends and family as half hippy, he loves the wild remoteness and rugged beauty of the Cornish coastline, where he walks, swims and meditates. He is a member of Mensa and of the International Society for Philosophical Enquiry.

Visit the author's website at:
www.jamescorfe.com

Also by this author

A BEAUTIFUL LOVE STORY
DEEPLY EROTIC
ATMOSPHERIC
SENSUOUS
UNUSUAL AND INTRIGUING
AND EXPECT THE UNEXPECTED!

A deeply erotic, sensuous and atmospheric journey through a beautiful love affair, set mainly in Cornwall in England.

David Bourne was a high flying London architect, who having lost his wife and little girl in a sudden tragic accident, has spent four years travelling the world trying to forget. He has just returned to England to start a new life in Cornwall, where he meets the beautiful Anna Redmond, the commander's wife.

See it through their eyes and feel it through their minds as it deepens and when the commander enters the arena, expect the unexpected! An unusual story and so real, it is thought-provoking and told with a great beauty woven into both the sadness and the joy.

Also by this author

An unusual and intriguing story

Hanna is a beautiful Scandinavian academic who finds herself subtly approached to compromise her integrity to facilitate a life changing promotion for her career driven husband.

From that point on, nothing can be the same. Whatever decision she makes, even if she makes no response at all, by virtue of the proposal being made, consequences are inevitable.

What would *you* do?

See it through her eyes and experience it through her mind as she makes her choices and the wheels of fate are set in motion. It is an unusual story of loyalty, of betrayal, and of love in its different forms. It is atmospheric and sensuous and with an ending you would not have foreseen.

REVIEW FOR *The Affairs Of The Commander's Wife*

"

The writer writes with great sensitivity both of the human mind and the human physique. The book is deeply erotic tempered with a greater need to understand and be part of another human's experiences. The writer shows appreciation and compassion. The book was a compelling read leaving the reader wanting to know the eventual outcome. It made one think!

REVIEW FOR *Hannah's Dilemma*

"

The book demonstrates man's ruthless exploitation of other human beings to attain his goal. I found it at times anger making and leaving me wishing to find out what will happen next. It was thought provoking, sensitively sensual and the writer displays a deep understanding of human nature. I thoroughly enjoyed it!

Chapter 1

I first met Alexander Reeme some two years ago. He is by definition a recruitment consultant, but in his own right, he would better be described as a head-hunter and mine was a head that he hunted.

He came to my gym occasionally. Whilst I am a regular attendee – two or three times a week – he would come just once in a while, having his own regular gym nearer to his home. He told me that he went to other gyms as a guest occasionally to get some variation in his routine but I also thought that it was for the possibility of making new contacts for his work. We had made eye contact a few times which we acknowledged with a smile and a nod and on one occasion when we were close, he spoke.

"You give those machines more justice than I," he said, his smile warming further. "Are you working to a programme?"

"Not really. I tend to follow some routine but of my own making. I do what I consider is necessary to try and maintain the shape that I have and I'm told it's good for the circulation," I replied returning his smile.

"So you are your own personal trainer."

"Absolutely."

"You're keeping your body toned and it shows. You look to be in pretty good shape. I'm just trying to slow down the inevitable," he replied. "When I look in the mirror, regardless of what I see, it would be worse if I didn't do anything."

"Profound," I told him.

We seemed to have an affinity. I'm not part of the social scene in the gym. I keep myself to myself pretty much as I do in my life generally. The typical conversation of the gym, the changing rooms and the showers, is not my scene - nought to sixty times, betting odds, the attributes of women or the bragging of deals made but I interact well and do have a few fellow gym users with whom I have the occasional chat and Alexander Reeme became one of them.

"Alexander Reeme," said he extending his hand. "Alex."

"Matt Rochester," I replied, offering mine.

"You're a regular," said he in a kindly way. "I generally see you here on my occasional visits. My regular is a gym nearer to my home."

"In London?"

"Yes, Chelsea."

"Not too far from here."

"No, but I like to get out a bit – new faces, different social scene and the bar and restaurant here is pretty good. I look upon my fellow gym participants – the likes of you – with envy."

"I look upon them with distain. It saddens me that they have no more meaningful way of useful recreation than I do."

"Explain," said he with a curious smile.

"Most are caught in the treadmill that is the routine grind of modern life and in their spare time they come here to actively run on a treadmill."

Alex laughed, appreciative of the observation.

"I'm haunted by the hideous sound of the machine – the constant whirring of the motor driving the belt and the pounding of the feet thumping a monotonous regular beat like a kettle drum."

"I know what you mean. It's the sound of the gym."

"It varies slightly between users. With a subtle ear you can distinguish without looking, between he who runs with ease and he who labours. One is almost driving the belt, the other is being driven. But whichever, it's a monotonous, relentless whirr and beat that haunts the sensitive mind. It is as a metronome to their daily routine – a fitting music score, as a lament is to a funeral. And it bores me. I tone up my body but risk ending up brain dead."

Alex laughed as not before. "Maybe some headphones with classical music might divert the brain."

"No. that wouldn't fit. My brain would see through it. 'Chariots of Fire' maybe. Mm, that's a thought – inject some sense of purpose, some passion into it."

Alex was highly amused. "Am I talking to a psychologist or a poet maybe?"

"Not quite. I'm a barrister. The next best thing," I added in jest.

"Good with words and nails the situation with the use of metaphors, analogies, shrewd observation and awareness. I would love to hear some of your examinations in court – the way you see things and elucidate them. You should produce a DVD."

"Are you a producer?"

"No. I'm a procurer. Reeme Associates – human resources. But independently, in my own right, I personally source the right person for the right job and vice versa. At the highest levels."

"A head hunter!"

"Believe it!" said he which together with his facial expression and tone of voice made one aware of his direction of purpose and self-belief.

I had heard of Reeme Associates – they were well known and here was the man himself. His regular business was in human resources – management recruitment through a number of offices throughout the country. It is very successful and that activity alone has made him a wealthy man. But over and above this, in his own right, he is a head-hunter extraordinaire, targeting individuals he knows, for companies that engage him personally to find suitable candidates at the very highest level. His reputation precedes him and he is held in the highest regard.

I was to learn that this is his forte – his great love. He is exceptional at assessing people. He works with individuals and company heads and brings them together with precision. He is revered for his extraordinary talent but often reviled for his seemingly ruthless approach where poaching is involved. He is the go-to man for boardrooms seeking particular qualities and experience and above all a candidate to be the exact fit. He has the uncanny ability to introduce individuals who were not only capable of providing the exactness of expertise necessary but also able to fit the company ethos.

To facilitate this, he keeps 'a little black book' of people he has met with exceptional ability – outstanding individuals at the top of their game and over a broad range of occupations. Much like sports or entertainment agents, he keeps in touch with them on a regular basis. They are basically social calls but with a clear purpose of checking if they are still happy in their present situation and whether they are still being adequately rewarded?

He lives on his wits. As a chef's reputation is only as good as his last meal, so Alexander Reeme's reputation is only as good as his last placement but he thrives on it. He relishes the challenge. Once tasked, he is a man on a mission. His fees for his personal skills are eye-watering. If he is a rich man from his routine consultancy, he is made very much richer by his personal individual introductions.

He wasn't your average gym participant. In his fifties, he looked to be in pretty good shape for his age and had a distinguished air about him both in his manner and his appearance. Not over tall, probably approaching six feet and not obviously overweight but his waistline giving the impression of being well nourished. His hair, now greying, curled slightly as it breached his collar. He wouldn't spend too much time on the apparatus – sufficient to justify his being there and to contribute to his wellbeing but not sufficient that he was on a mission or dedicated to obtaining a new image. He broke sweat but not on a sustained basis. He dressed for the gym but smartly as to engage the social scene rather than for continued exertion. He would spend as much time in observation as using the equipment and was generally to be seen with his towel around his neck and his hands holding each end from just above his waist.

"Apart from court work do you specialise?" he asked

"I'm taking more of a back room function nowadays. Courtrooms interest me less now. I don't enjoy the challenge as much as I used to. There's always the odd courtroom visit to make – some cases I have to accept but basically I only take on something if it particularly interests me."

"You say back room. Contracts? Do you specialise in contracts?"

"Yes, very much so. With properly drawn up contracts there are fewer court cases. And I do a lot of advisory work. I can exercise my reasoning without the courtroom theatrics."

His interest was aroused immediately and he turned into me so as to speak in earnest. "Look, I'd like to get to know you better and there is something I'd like to show you – take your opinion on. Can I buy you some lunch in the club?"

I liked him. He was certainly very different from the average club member and he obviously had something on his mind. "Yes, why not?" I said. "I'm intrigued and I'd enjoy your company. I spend quite a bit of time alone these days."

"Have you done in here?" he asked.

"Yes – you?"

"Lunch would be a sufficient excuse even if I wasn't!" he replied with a wry smile.

We made our way to the changing rooms, showered and went to the bar to peruse the menus.

He had a particularly likeable way of engaging – profound but often with a humour built in. "Feel free to select something from the top end. Even if your lunch is fifty quid and I have you for an hour and a half, I'd say that could under value you by some several hundred pounds at least."

"But this is predominantly social and you can't put a price on the right company," I said.

"What do you fancy?"

"Well I'm going to considerably under-value myself and have a sandwich – or baguettes I think they are."

"I'll join you," said Alex. The way they do them here it's more like up-market pub grub."

We chatted away saying something of ourselves and I really did like him. He was shrewd but seemed honest and had depth. His demeanour was of great confidence and I suspected he had every reason to be so. These characteristics showed and I could understand why he was trusted and highly successful. When we had finished eating and had coffees in front of us, he told me of a problem he had encountered – one that crops up quite regularly apparently.

"I had a highly suitable and financially rewarding position for a brilliant engineer that I have in my book," said Alex looking into me. "But his present employer said he was bound by his contract and if I tried to extract him, they would take me to court. He was currently working on highly sensitive projects and was vital to their continuance." He went to his bag, pulled out some papers and put them in front of me. "That is a copy of his contract. I'm not asking you for formal professional advice but just to peruse it and give me your thoughts."

5

It ran to just three pages. I put on my reading glasses and quickly perused it. I lowered my head and looked to him above my glasses.

"It's awful! It has so little substance as to be virtually meaningless."

"Could it have been deliberately worded loosely to allow for interpretation to benefit the company in differing circumstances?"

"No. It's not that clever. It doesn't benefit anyone. It's just badly written – it's atrocious!"

"Do you see that sort of thing often?"

"Yes, too often. Look, poaching, so called, is in itself not illegal and in any event how do you define poaching. He is entitled to be made aware of other positions either by advertisement or word of mouth. It's his decision. So they can't take you to court for that reason and if he was that vital to the company and the projects on which he was working, he should be subject to a contract far better than this," I said, gesticulating with the contract. "There should be post-termination restrictions as part of the contract. It should include restrictive covenants that specify precisely what he can and cannot do." I gave him some idea of the type of clauses that should be considered and some guidance on their limitations. "The company has a right to protect its interests but it must allow the employee his rights.

"But in your line of work," I went on, "you must be familiar with much of this and it must crop up from time to time."

"Absolutely. This was just a case in point," he qualified, gesturing to the contract.

At his level he must have considerable knowledge of contracts generally and it must crop up on a regular basis and the contract he had shown me was too basic and too flawed to warrant serious discussion and I realised it was simply a means of enabling a debate. In effect it formed the basis of an interview. He was interviewing me – sounding me out. I thought it was possibly carried around in his briefcase for just such a purpose. He was seeking either someone that he could turn to when situations arise or he was looking for a lawyer to fill a particular position.

We talked for some while, concentrating on employment contracts with employees of a very senior nature and on sensitive projects and also on more general contracts on supplies and collaborations. He was listening intently. His elbows were on the arms of his chair with his hands together with his two index fingers together and touching his lips with his head slightly turned but his eyes were looking into me. I could picture his brain in overdrive.

"May I ask your age Matt? I'm fifty six – I can give you around two decades I guess."

I nodded. "I'm thirty five."

He sat back in his chair and held up a finger vertically, aligning to me like a gun sight. "I know people at a high level who would very much like to talk to you," he said. "There could be work for you from time to time and on a very well paid basis. Basically name your price – within reason of course. Might that interest you?"

"Yes I think it might. But I don't work for the con artists. I don't draw up contracts that attempt to make the illegal legal."

"I know you don't. Your integrity is most apparent and that is part of the attraction. When you know who I am talking about you will understand that."

My details went into his little black book and he said he would be in touch shortly.

"How was the lunch?" he asked.

"Very good. My chambers would be horrified. I'm now taking payment in baguettes. I could imagine my clerk, the cheeky sod that he is, asking me if the banks provide special paying in slips for baguettes and would his salary similarly be paid in sustenance?"

Alex laughed. "Oh I'd love to hear you in court."

I was to begin a journey that would change my life and in a way that I couldn't have foreseen.

Chapter 2

Alex phoned me after a few days as promised and set up a meeting with a prospective client.

He had only our conversation over lunch to gauge my competence but it wouldn't be difficult for him to get knowledge of many of my court cases. Some were public knowledge, others could be accessed by people who know their way around these matters and I was sure he would have further verification of my abilities should he wish.

Work followed. It was indeed a very prestigious organisation and while the work was bread and butter to me, it was on occasions quite interesting with the type of operations in which they were involved.

Alex kept in touch and more than was necessary for professional reasons. We became friends. Very often his phone calls wouldn't mention work – they were purely social and I found him visiting my club more regularly and we would often enjoy a coffee or a drink in the bar depending on the time of day and sometimes have lunch together. I'm not a great social person – I live very much in my own world but I did value Alex's friendship.

Three months on, he telephoned me to say he had an opportunity for me that, as he put it, could be 'the mother of all opportunities' for a man of my calibre. But I had gone through a period of re-assessment of my life, of where I was now and what I wanted to do for the future.

"Alex, I am of course grateful for the consideration but I don't want to take on any more commitments now. I'm re-evaluating my life and making plans to do something different," I told him almost apologetically.

"Matt, this opportunity could be life changing in itself for a lawyer of your capability."

"Really Alex, I've done a lot of thinking recently. I have been unsettled and my desire for a change that has been brewing for some time now, has intensified and I'm going to alter course."

There was silence for a few moments as he digested my words and realised that there was a depth to what I was saying that he hadn't appreciated when I first spoke. "Matt, can we meet? Talk this through. Lunch? At your club perhaps."

"Yes. Yes of course. Good idea."

I obviously owed him an explanation and the telephone wasn't the way to do it. Apart from that I would perhaps like the opportunity of talking it through. While I was resolved now, having given it so much thought, I hadn't discussed it with anyone and to share some of my thinking with someone like Alex might, I thought, be helpful.

Lunch at my club again but I knew that this time was going to be very different.

"Matt," said Alex in emphasis as we met and whilst we shook hands he put his other arm around my shoulder. He knew this was to be a heart-to-heart and his gesture was one of great friendship.

We went to the bar and immediately ordered drinks but Alex having an outline of my thinking was anxious to get into meaningful conversation and that, for the time being, took precedence over the ordering of food. This was not simply a social get together it was to explain my future plans and that in itself suggested that it might define our future relationship.

"So Matt," said Alex, gesturing with his hands in emphasis of his eagerness to engage, "talk to me. Where are you now?"

"I'm making a life changing move. I'm going to find a place in this world where I can escape the known daily routine, where I can find space and peace in beautiful surroundings and preferably in a warm climate. And I want to write."

Alex was listening intently. I could sense the depth of his understanding but he couldn't help a timely aside. "To get off the treadmill. The reality one not the metaphorical one."

"Both," I stressed. If I am to run in my new found paradise I can assure you it won't be in a gym. Early morning along a beach is more likely."

"Do you have somewhere in mind?"

"I'm thinking Greek Islands."

"Permanently?"

I pursed my lips and swayed my head. "Open ended exploration but with no great expectation of returning as I feel at this time."

"So..." Alex was quick to respond but paused when I continued to speak.

"My need for change is great. I will either find a new direction or given time it may be a stepping stone. I think I would be more likely to move on than return."

"You're pretty well resolved. You say given time?" Have you given yourself a probationary period so to speak?"

"I suppose by the nature of the move there must be an exploratory period but I haven't defined it."

"You've not mentioned this before, Matt. I know you've cut back on your court work, become more back room as you say but I hadn't picked up on such a drastic change. Has it been quite sudden? Is there a particular reason?"

"No, it's not sudden. It's been developing for quite some time and there is no particular reason. It's just the person I am now I suppose. What or who I have become."

"A fish out of water!"

I smiled. "There's a certain irony in that remark." I chuckled. Alex couldn't know just how ironic it was. "As a teenager I had a friend in the west country. She lived on the Devon and Cornwall border and I spent a lot of time with her wild swimming and surfing. I got offers of entry from several top universities to study law. I chose Oxford, not solely because of its obvious kudos, but, well it was the nearest to my friend in the West Country. Whilst I was determined to immerse myself in my studies, it was not to be to the detriment of my spare time pursuits. Weekends, holidays, plus other times that weren't to be broadcast, were spent in the wild. My senior tutor saw fit to inform me that I had to decide whether my future was to be in a courtroom or on a surfboard. Again, as I saw it, the answer was both."

"Mm. However much time you spent in the sea, it didn't prevent you coming away with a first class honours degree," said Alex profoundly.

"I didn't find it too difficult to be honest. I took in the detail like machine code and I loved the debates, the reasoning and the use of language. Initially I was in my element in a courtroom, had successes and was eventually called to the bar. But it became routine, claustrophobic almost. More than that. I earnestly wanted justice – convict the guilty, free the innocent. But it wasn't quite that simple. I was even told that I shouldn't take it so seriously."

Alex was looking into me deeply. He was very thoughtful.

"You wanted more!"

"I wanted more!"

"Did you manage to keep up your surfing?"

"To a far lesser extent. London is much further away from the West Country so now it's a rare treat but some occasional wild swimming."

"Holidays?"

"I tend to go where it's warm now, like the Mediterranean. Surfing may have left me but the call of the wild, open spaces, seascapes and my vivid imagination haven't."

"Are you writing now?"

"Yes, bits and pieces. I know a publisher well and they have expressed interest to work with me. No guarantees but I primarily write for myself. To live in my imagination a life that reality can't provide so whilst it would be nice, publication is not the prime motive."

"You might step into that imaginary life on your Greek Island making your imagination and reality as one."

"I think that whatever reality I find, my imagination will always be a few steps ahead."

"That's very profound. A man of your intellect –well I find you pretty unique. One might assume that a courtroom would be the ideal scenario for you to exercise it, but I've come to know you differently. You're a very unusual man Matt and I can understand your thinking. Tell me, I know you have a partner, is she eager to make the change with you?"

"Actually Alex, we're estranged – have been for some while…" Alex suddenly became aware of someone eavesdropping – the bar was filling up and we no longer had privacy.

"Look, shall we find a table and order some food – continue with privacy?"

We bagged a spare table away from the bar in an alcove and ordered some lunch.

"I'm sorry Matt – I didn't know. Is that part of your decision to start afresh?"

"It's ok Alex, I haven't spoken about it because again, it's not something new. It's been a gradual process over several years."

"You've grown apart," suggested Alex, showing keenness to understand this further aspect of my situation.

"Yes. Yes we have. We met during our university years. She didn't go to Oxford but she was near enough for us to meet up quite regularly – she had a car courtesy of wealthy parents. We got on really well as students, me studying law, her accountancy. Both academics really and we moved along together."

"Did she share your love of the ocean for recreation?"

"No. she wasn't a bad swimmer and did come wild swimming with me on occasions and we did a lot of country walking together but she was no surfer. When we'd both finished university we shared a small flat together in London. That facilitated the career prospects that we both had and for the first few years it was great. But as time passed we began to see life differently. She was really career minded almost to the exclusion of all else and with me expressing some disenchantment with my court work and finding my artistic side and my imagination playing a greater part in my conversations, it didn't reconcile with her total 'heads down' focus as she was moving quickly up the corporate ladder."

"She's obviously good at what she does."

"Yes she is but also she has a disposition that makes her desirable in that world. She wasn't short of job offers and eventually she took a job that was offered to her in Singapore. Her mother was of Singapore extraction so there were connections and an obvious leaning on her part. It was for three months initially with a then possible return to the London operation. We still had a relationship but understandably it was conducted in more difficult circumstances."

We paused as the food was brought to our table. No baguettes this time. Alex had fish and chips with mushy peas, something he doesn't have too often apparently. It took him back to his younger years he said, albeit that now it was served on fine tableware and linen tablecloths rather than from newspaper. I had a pasta.

As we started to eat, Alex gestured for me to continue. He was clearly eager to learn more of my situation and where it might fit in to my new direction.

"Towards the end of the three months she was offered a permanent senior position in Singapore which she took. It certainly made her a high flyer with all the trimmings that went with it. She couldn't refuse. It was the position for which she was destined and her culture made her a good fit."

Alex was still listening intently and nodding his head in understanding. "How often would she return home?" he asked.

"Quite often actually. Trips to London were fairly frequent – routine meet-ups and conferences as well as pretty generous leave. But the relationship changed. Her head really was locked into her elevated position and the world in which she then operated and whilst we were both capable of a meaningful conversation embracing our different professions, our vision, our world view if you like, showed disparity.

"So your relationship. Did it just peter out or did you have a discussion about it?"

"It took its own course, we accepted who we were and where we were and a discussion wouldn't alter anything so it's best avoided. Having virtually gone through university together and the formative maturing years that followed, we obviously had an affinity and an active sex life but as our time together lessened and with our altered outlook, both the emotional and the physical aspects changed. We were growing apart. As time moved on we met more as loving friends rather than lovers. We had sex, we didn't make love. And it became more clinical, concluded in what the surveys tell us is the average time taken – twelve minutes is it? Eventually we did have that discussion and we had to agree that we led different lives. We had grown apart. I think she now has a new relationship in Singapore."

"And you Matt? No new relationship?" I shook my head. "No outlet? Looking as you do, your intellect, your bearing, you've got to be so attractive to women. I would have thought they would be lined up."

I laughed. "Thanks for the vote of confidence Alex. There are always opportunities obviously. I have female colleagues and the occasional date. I generally prefer female company to male but I'm not into casual sex."

"Yes, I can understand that Matt. You're a sensitive guy. I hope you find someone soon. Women are important for all of us. Female company is a vital cog in the wheel of the universe,"

"I like the way you put that Alex. Profound! But you're a lucky man. You have a lovely wife – very attractive."

"Oh! Have you met her?"

"No but I've seen her from a distance. Twice actually. I saw her through the window when she collected you from here once and I also, by coincidence, saw you out walking together in Chelsea from across the road."

"You find her attractive?"

"Very. Elegance and maturity…"

"You like maturity?"

"Very much so, I'm not into young girls."

He nodded thoughtfully… "So what about your work here – the back room stuff as you call it. Will you continue with it?"

"Yes. Most of it is online, so with a laptop and a half decent internet connection it gives me great flexibility."

"Greek taverna, even the shade of a palm fringed beach should you go further afield," said Alex elucidating the flexibility. "Tell me, have you mentioned your plans to 'The Group?'" as Alex refers to the organisation he put me in touch with.

"No, not yet. There's time for that once my plans come to fruition and I wouldn't do that until I had discussed it all with you. I would want to have made you fully aware before I discuss it with them."

"Thanks, I appreciate that. I don't foresee a problem," said Alex. "I know how much they value your work. They would want to fit in so far as it is feasible."

"Most of that work is online now, so that wouldn't change and if it is the Mediterranean, the telephone would work and I could easily make trips to the UK. I would keep their work and a selection of my existing connections but I will relinquish some of it to give myself more time and space."

"So the mother of all opportunities is not going to entice you is it?"

"I'm afraid not Alex but I am truly grateful to you for the opportunity and for our continuing friendship."

"Do you know Matt, knowing you as I do now, I say good for you! I'm pleased for you and I wish you well. Obviously we must keep in touch for connections, but especially as friends.

"How was the fish and chips?"

"Lovely! And nowadays it comes with tartare sauce!"

Chapter 3

My phone rang. It was Alex and so soon – just a few days after our open hearted lunch. It had to be a follow up on our discussion.

"Alex. Hello!"

"Hello Matt, how are you?" That wasn't his usual hello. He could have said many things that felt normal but asking me how I was after just a few days wasn't one of them.

"Yes I'm fine Alex, are you?"

"Matt, I'd like to have another chat with you in private."

"You're not going to try to change my mind on 'the mother of all opportunities' are you? I'm pretty resolved on that one and already into my research of likely destinations."

"No far from it. In fact it's your new plans I'd like to talk to you about. But as I say, I'd like to talk to you in private and somewhere quiet where we won't be disturbed."

His whole approach was different from the Alex that I had come to know and his proposal suggested that he had something unusual and very personal that he wanted to discuss. "Do you have somewhere in mind Alex?"

"I know a hotel just a few miles out that has a nice restaurant in addition to its bar area. I use it from time to time and they would save us a table in a quiet part. The restaurant doesn't get too busy lunchtimes anyway."

"When do you have in mind?"

"Would this coming Monday suit you? I know it's short notice but it would suit me well."

An unusual greeting on the phone, so soon after our recent lunch, the need for privacy and I sensed an urgency to his proposal. What could be on his mind? "Yes. Yes, I'll make myself available Alex."

"Excellent. Look if I use a taxi, I could pick you up on the way and we travel together. It will only be about a twenty minute journey from your neck of the woods. That way it saves the hassle of cars and we can enjoy a glass or two of a good wine, not having to drive afterwards"

Monday was soon upon us and we travelled to the hotel chatting of everyday matters. We were shown to a table in the corner of the restaurant which had the privacy that Alex sought. He ordered a bottle of wine and I awaited the reason for our meeting.

"I was sorry to hear that your long term relationship is over, Matt. I sense that it has affected you more than you're letting on. That maybe it is more of a factor in your decision to go for a completely fresh start. Oh I know you don't give up a career as a barrister because of a broken relationship. Obviously, as you say, the career change has been coming for some while but I do sense that perhaps the nature and the timing of your plans are in some way influenced by your split."

I thought deeply to give him an honest answer. "Not the split in itself, Alex. Our relationship had run its course and acceptance had embedded. It wasn't the traumatic end of a love affair, and it wasn't one-sided. There was mutual acceptance and of course a sadness but it wasn't a life changing experience. If anything it is the absence of a relationship that has come to bear, rather than the ending of a previous one. I do love female company. It balances my hormones, fills the empty half of my psyche." I leaned to him somewhat and in softened tones added, "And if it is in a relationship, it is all the more meaningful. I feel complete."

"Fulfilled."

"Yes, in a word. So yes the restlessness in my career and my urban lifestyle is compounded with a loneliness."

"And you say you are not into casual relationships."

"It would have to have some meaning. I'm not into one night stands. Sex for me is very emotional as well as physical and a one or two night stands are not a good fit. I'm sure they would be better suited to the not long sexually activated opportunistic college student, or the state of the art hormone induced play away from home male stereotype."

Alex chuckled. "Matt… I haven't said up to now but Jennifer and I are also estranged. I did think about telling you at our lunch the other day but I thought it might detract from your revelation as to where you are now. The discussion was primarily about you, but having thought about things and knowing you now as I

17

do, it's something I can share with you – in the strictest confidence of course. I know I can trust you."

"The confidence goes without saying, Alex…" I gestured with my hands re-enforcing my words. "I'm sorry, I obviously didn't know. How long?"

He clenched his lips as he considered his answer. "Must be four or five years now."

"When you say estranged…"

He interrupted me. "We lead separate lives now, meeting periodically as friends. I still have her welfare at heart and she mine. There is still some affinity there – we go back quite a way. Divorce is not an option. Neither of us has expressed a desire for that and there are…" he hesitated to find the words, "private reasons why that is not likely to happen – certainly in the foreseeable future."

"You seem reconciled to the situation."

"Yes we both are. I'll be honest with you Matt, I too like female company – I adore it!"

He had virtually admitted to having affairs or even possibly a new interest. I have come across that before, where for various reasons people want to remain married but ostensibly have new partners. It seemed that might be the case here. But then came the next revelation that I hadn't in any way anticipated or even suspected.

"Actually Matt I…" again he hesitated but this time as if considering whether he should divulge his thoughts. He leaned to me and in a lowered voice he said, "I… I also like male company. Actually I'm bi-sexual." That did surprise me. I had no idea and no reason to suppose. "I'm not officially out, as it were, so I trust that this too is in confidence," said he, entreating me with his eyes.

"It goes without saying Alex," I confirmed, holding out my hands to again reinforce this.

"The trust is a measure of the esteem in which I hold you and value you as a friend," he said in earnest.

"I presume Jennifer knows."

"Oh yes! Jennifer has known for… well, a long time. She is not in any way critical and in some respects has been supportive but it makes for an altered relationship on her part. We no longer have a physical relationship."

"Is that a problem for you – I mean the absence of that side of things with her?"

"I would continue it but she is unable to do that since I am active both ways if you understand and she never was highly sexed anyway. In fact I would say that she is under inclined that way, which to me is somewhat ironic as she is highly attractive in all aspects and is never short of admirers and increasingly so since she is older.. And that includes you from what you say."

I nodded my head. "I certainly thought her highly attractive both physically and as the person I suspect she is."

Alex too was nodding in approval now. "I know of several men who have made no secret of their attraction to her and at least two of them that I know of have come on to her."

"And you don't think she is interested!"

"I think not."

"Even in the absence of a relationship in her marriage?"

"Yes."

"Is she career minded?"

"Yes, or was. Less so now."

"What does she do?"

"Art history – interiors. She used to be a magazine editor but she now mainly writes articles. She's quite high profile – look her up. But that doesn't take the place of sex or even a relationship of her own. If anything I would have thought it may have given her opportunities."

"I'm sure looking as she does there must have been opportunities."

"Yes, I'm sure too."

"Do you think you would have known if she'd had a relationship? "

"Most probably. I wouldn't say she wears her heart on her sleeve as it were but she is quite open as a person and her emotions show on the outside to someone who knows her as I do. But look, Jennifer is her own person – very much in charge of herself. She is not going to do anything that she doesn't want to do, she is not going to be used and she would have no hesitation in putting someone down if needs be."

19

We paused as our food was put before us. Such was the intensity of our conversation that it took its arrival to remind us that we'd ordered it and before that, ordered and sampled the wine.

"So Matt, have you found a location for your new adventure yet?"

"No, I've considered one or two possibilities but haven't decided."

"Still thinking Greek Islands?"

"Yes. I like Greece – climate, cuisine, the people, culture and of course the amazing history. It's very beautiful and there are some quiet locations to be found."

"Will you buy a place there?"

"If I found the right place but I think I'll rent initially, give myself time to acclimatise and be in a better position to find the right place to buy when I'm settled."

Alex was giving me the same look he was giving me when he first offered me the possibility of work with his contacts. His demeanour betrayed his intention. He zeroed in on me raising a finger vertically in front of my face like a gunsight as before. He was going to make a suggestion or even an offer.

"How would you feel if I said I know of something that may suit you?" he said, enticing a response.

"Go on."

"It's not the Greek Islands, it's mainland Greece, east coast, beautiful quiet spot, off the main tourist track, somewhat midway between Athens and Thessaloniki. Beautiful remote coastline, cliffs, coves and of course the Aegean Sea."

I was intrigued. "Go on."

"A lovely place to stay. Ideal I would have thought for your purpose. Certainly initially. Not a hotel, it's basically a taverna with rooms. It's on the coast, by the harbour of a very small town or large village. It's very much a traditional Greek taverna that, from what I understand, hasn't changed much over the years, catering for the local clientele – not tourist driven. Quintessential Greece. There is a decent phone signal in the area and internet connection is pretty decent."

"Sounds very interesting."

"Prices are cheap there and the owner and most of the staff speak some English. Ideal for a prolonged stay and I think they'd do some sort of deal. It's the sort of place you come across by accident rather than by research."

"You seem to know it well – you've been there?"

"Not exactly but it sounds the ideal place to immerse oneself in another culture."

"It sounds great. It's fuelling my imagination. How do you know of it?"

He ignored my question and continued, "And Matt, there's a bonus!" `

"A bonus?"

"A chance at Jennifer!"

"A chance at Jennifer?"

He just looked at me with a subtle smile and nodded. I felt a jolt internally that must have shown in my eyes. With all my years in the legal profession, one could be forgiven for thinking they had heard it all but I confess to not seeing that one coming and I understood now, that for his revelations and this proposal, why he wanted absolute privacy both for the location and our seating arrangement.

"Are you suggesting I could have a holiday there with Jennifer?"

"No. what I'm suggesting is far more subtle. Let me explain. Jennifer has bought a villa in the area that needs complete renovation – a long term project. She's now staying at the taverna until it becomes habitable."

I had to smile – a smile of intrigue. "And you'd write a letter of introduction for me."

"No, no, no! That wouldn't work. I'm not at all certain that she would be interested. No, as I have said, it is quite subtle. You both happen to be staying at the same remote place in a beautiful location and your paths are bound to cross in one way or another. You would either get to know one another or you wouldn't – if and how it develops is the unknown. But it's a virtual holiday situation in a warm climate and as the old saying goes – the likes of you with the likes of her. She's not been interested in the previous opportunities that I know about and as I said, I get the impression that she is not generally interested anyway. But you are different – good looking, your build, your intellect and your personality. I would have thought you are absolutely her type – younger, around ten or twelve years and vice-versa for you. If she has made any comments about men they are usually younger and you like maturity. I would be utterly intrigued – would she or wouldn't she?"

"And if she does, where would that leave you and me?"

"Potentially the same as we are now."

"Potentially yes but there must be an element of risk."

"The risk is part of it – for me anyway. It's the adrenalin factor. It's for real isn't it! I don't play games."

I too was intrigued, not as to whether Jennifer would or wouldn't but by the situation on offer. My first thoughts were, 'why haven't I turned it down by now?' and the answer to that was quite simple – the wheels were still turning in my mind.

"You haven't turned it down yet," said Alex with a look on his face of someone expecting to close a deal, and that all that was needed now was a nod and a handshake. Except that it wasn't a deal. It wasn't even an understanding. He had found a place and a location that ostensibly was ideal for my plans and there was the factor that in that location, his wife may or may not be available depending on purely natural occurrences with no strings attached or indeed expectations. He had all but headhunted me for his wife but in intriguing circumstances.

"So would you be giving me your blessing or just turning a blind eye?"

"Whatever may happen doesn't need to be blessed and if I turn a blind eye, I might miss out on some of the stimulation," said he profoundly.

He took a piece of paper that was folded from his pocket and slid it across the table to me. Inside was the location, the name of the taverna, the name of the owner, telephone number, and email address.

"They have a website," he added, "but it's very basic and it is mostly in Greek. It's more for local reference than for pulling in tourists. You can't book or pay online. If you phone, they will almost certainly answer in Greek but if you speak English they will respond. Don't mention me of course – you'd have to think about how you heard of them. Anything you'd like to ask Matt?"

"Do you have any children?"

Alex gave a little sigh of resignation. "No. Jennifer is unable."

"Why do you want Jennifer suited, Alex?"

"Purely intrigue. I want to know whether she would, and if she does, knowing her as I do, I would find the sexual and emotional aspects of her affair stimulating."

"If I do go there Matt, it would be primarily for the location and the venue. I wouldn't go in anticipation of an affair with your wife, however willing you might be."

He put his hands up to me expressing acceptance. I accept that but the opportunity would be there by default, wouldn't it! And again I note that you haven't turned it down yet."

"No, to my own surprise, I haven't turned it down yet Alex! I'm still turning it over."

"Good Matt. Continue to do that! More wine?"

Chapter 4

The thrust of the seat on my back as the aircraft's engines are opened to full throttle, the change of sensation as the wheels leave the runway followed by the sudden upward surge is exhilarating. For me, as an experience when flying, it is matched only by the sense of relief when the wheels are felt to touch the ground again on the destination runway. I'm told that even many seasoned travellers still breathe a subconscious sigh of relief too.

The three and a half hour flight to Thessaloniki was a time of reflection, a period of calm after my hectic preparations to get away as soon as possible. Once I had started to think seriously about Greece and research possible destinations, my daily routine was purgatory. The day of reckoning beckoned. I was where I didn't want to be and the long anticipated lifestyle change became urgent. My back-room work – mainly contracts and legal opinions – didn't have to be done in a back room. A warm climate, seascapes and beautiful surroundings, provided good internet connections were available, would serve just as well and that is where I wanted to be to enable my imagination and my creative instinct to flourish.

As if by some miraculous intervention by the governing powers of this world, Alexander Reeme not only arrived on the scene but came up with a highly suitable location and facility that very closely resembled what I was looking for but to date, hadn't been able to find. My research on that part of Eastern Greece and the specific location confirmed its appeal and a check on the taverna's website showing its local authenticity rather than as a tourist mecca convinced me to give it a go and I got to work on it straight away.

Preparations were hectic – making new arrangements with the work sources that I was keeping on and organising my apartment for prolonged absence. I had no second thoughts. Having made my decision to go, my head was down and there were no idle moments that may have allowed doubts to intrude. As the plane settled into its cruising mode, the journey well underway, I felt at peace. I was in transition and a calmness enveloped me. There was no turning back now and I was eager to embrace the new lifestyle that I sought.

And Jennifer Reeme? Intrigue and that is all there was. I wasn't ruling her out but neither was she ruled in. If Alex had emphasised the chance of an affair with his wife in any other circumstances I wouldn't have been interested. That would never have been the priority – my lifestyle change was the key factor. For Alex I sensed the priority was different. Oh, he was pleased to be of help in offering a suitable location and venue that he knew of and I'm sure he would have told me about it even if his wife had no connection with it. But I was in no doubt that my possible involvement with his wife was more of an interest to him than my finding a suitable place for my new life. Could I foresee problems there? Yes, is the short answer. In my profession I can't help being aware of possible scenarios but I wasn't intent on pursuing that aspect and even if I did, there is the strong possibility that she would not be interested so I hadn't considered the possible shortcomings too deeply.

Would I like sex with Jennifer Reeme? In my mind yes, bring it on but in reality I'm not so sure. My mind is as fertile as the next man's – maybe more so. My imagination is highly active and couple this with my absence of a relationship for some while and my loneliness and I could become very creative in that area but however desirable it might be to exercise it, I am careful to keep that private. To do otherwise would see me out of character. Some psychologists and psychiatrists say we should act out our fantasies – to clear out possible bottlenecks in the system. I have had many conversations in that regard over the years, particularly in some of the cases I have handled but even if I thought it desirable, I don't walk on thin ice.

I did look Jennifer up and as Alex had said, she was quite high profile. She has a website with her career details and her areas of speciality both in Art history and interior design, listing some of the projects in which she has been involved and also testimonials from some of her clients. She has been on television a number of times, both in her own right and also featured on other programs. There was a photograph of her, head and shoulders, which showed her much as I remembered her in profile from my fleeting glimpses but what it also did was to show me the character in her face that I couldn't get from a distance. She looked arty but with a depth. She appeared to me as what I have heard described as thinking man's crumpet. She was classy.

Airports are airports but from the aircraft's windows, foreign airports always look different from their UK counterparts to me. Is it the sunshine, the light, the people, or is it simply the mind knowing it is a far away destination. It was early May and the bright warm sunshine was very welcoming.

I had hired a car. I was recommended to a smaller firm who offered slightly older cars, albeit in excellent condition but at a better price and booking it for a month, with an option to renew, got me a very good deal. I got a good sized sporty Volvo hatchback, five years old which gave me a bit of street cred. I wasn't immediately an obvious tourist, blending in more with the local scene – even more so when it got a layer of dust on it.

The drive south from Thessaloniki was two hours plus, with motorways for much of the early part of the journey, running parallel to the east coast – fast cruising with stunning glimpses of the Aegean Sea. The last part of the journey was on smaller roads at a more leisurely pace, winding through several mountain villages as this was an area where the high ground extended almost to the coast.

Greece is traditionally known for its whitewashed buildings and blue paintwork. My time in Greece has mainly been spent on the Cycladic islands, which are particularly known for this feature with almost all the buildings in conformity. There are many reasons given for the origins of this tradition, starting with the 'Preference of the ancient gods.' This is considered a myth, the more likely reason being less romantic. In the nineteenth century it was decreed that all buildings should be painted white to try and reduce the effects of a major cholera outbreak. Lime wash was used which was considered to be antibacterial and made the buildings cooler, which in turn made the insides less of a breeding ground. I understand the blue colour was introduced in the late 1960's by the then government to give a uniformity and assimilate with the Greek flag. While this was subsequently relaxed the tradition has been maintained by many by choice – it certainly looks quite stunning in the sunlight and is firmly in the minds of tourists. The mainland is less steeped in that tradition with more natural stonework to be seen alongside those painted white. The mountain villages in particular have a fair number of natural stone buildings with the old woodwork naturally weathered and unpainted and they are very beautiful.

My destination didn't disappoint – a large village typical of those in the area, the main street lined with an assortment of artisan shops in traditional buildings and stalls. It was so characterful and I drove slowly taking it in until my taverna appeared ahead by the small harbour front, the sea becoming clearly visible. It was easily recognisable both from the website and by its location. It was a sprawling building, the stonework painted white with the old wooden windows, shutters and doors having been painted blue many years ago, now left to weather, giving a patina of faded blue here and there blending artistically with weathered natural wood. It was old and very characterful. Outside were some trees and well-established shrubs in flower covering part of the walls with many tables and chairs dotted between them and along a side passage with a number of people sitting at them even though it was then late afternoon.

I parked on some open ground at the side that served as a car park and made my way inside. My first thoughts were an extension to my thoughts on the outside. Wow! It gave the impression of being the sort of place that you stumble upon while touring in the middle of nowhere that looks foreign in the extreme. It was a large open area with a bar down one side with many assorted tables and chairs scattered throughout, leaving a clear space – I presumed for music and dancing in front of the long bar. Again there were many large shrubs in planters, smaller ones in pots dotted throughout and a series of blackboards on one wall with dozens of meals and snacks chalked on them, some partly rubbed out and smudged here and there. It was mainly in Greek but I recognised some English and if it could be read at all, there was so much up there it would take a long time to do so. Even at this time of day there must have been thirty or more customers, some seated some standing or on stools at the bar and several staff coming and going.

You would not expect English to be spoken and indeed any conversation that could be heard was in Greek. One could feel alien there. The regular tourist could easily find it daunting but to the discerning traveller it was an absolute gem. The décor and the atmosphere in general was a time warp from the nineteen thirties or before even with no modernisation apparent. It all looked totally natural, not pretentious or touristy in any way and I felt enthusiastic about my stay

"Hello. Matt Rochester," I said, presenting myself to the very Greek looking lady behind the bar, expecting her to understand some English. "I have a room reserved."

She smiled. "We expect you. I tell Maya."

Maya Costopolou was the Owner who I spoke to on the phone when I made the booking. Within a minute or two she came to the bar and walked round to meet me with a lovely welcoming smile on her face and an outstretched hand. "Hello Mr Rochester," she said warmly, "I am Maya. Welcome to our taverna," she added as we shook hands.

She was of late middle age nicely presented, not unattractive and was charming with a confidence about her. Her English was very good albeit with quite a strong Greek accent which I remembered from the phone call.

"It's lovely to be here. Please call me Matt," I replied.

"This is Maria," she said, turning to the lady behind the bar that I spoke to on arrival, who smiled coyly in response.

"Hi, I'm Matt" I told her too.

"Did you have a good journey?" asked Maya.

"Yes thank you. It's been a long day but worth it I feel. I particularly enjoyed the last part through the mountains. It was beautiful."

"Plenty of places for you to explore," she replied still smiling broadly. "I will take you to your room," she continued and we made our way to the double doors at the back of the room beyond the bar, through which were the stairs to the first floor. It was a very wide staircase rising in two stages with a flat horizontal section ahead of us halfway between the flights as it turned at right angles twice, leading to a meandering corridor serving the rooms on that floor.

She opened a door and invited me to walk in. "I hope this is ok for you." she said.

I was pleasantly surprised. The room was quite spacious and light enough from the one window that looked out onto the main street of the village. Again the room was a time warp from a bygone age, with few, if any, modern updates but for the electrical wiring which I could see was more recent and the creation of a small en-suite shower room. The furniture was simple but adequate and the drapes and bedcover were in a pale drab green colour which, with the plain bare walls, gave a cool if sombre atmosphere. The walls, part bare stone, part rendered but unevenly so, looked to have been painted many years ago but have weathered, having a patina of light and darker misting over their entirety. It was the sort of look that people pay good money to interior designers to achieve but this was completely natural, created by time whilst being left alone – the real thing! The floor had its wooden boards exposed, again looking naturally distressed with a couple of mats strategically located. My first thought was that it had probably not changed much, if at all, since the second world war, eighty or so years ago when the Germans were in occupation here. If a film of that period were to be made here, they probably wouldn't need to change a thing and that goes for the downstairs as well. In truth it was just what I was hoping for – natural, neutral and unpretentious and it looked very clean. I wasn't stepping into a design cliché from a particular decade of the second half of the last century or the commercial come corporate hotel décor and furniture and colour schemes of the current century.

"It's very nice," I said sincerely, turning to her.

"Now look," said Maya, There is a larger room with a sea view that will be free in about two to three weeks from now and it has a nice desk by the window which may be ideal for your writing if you are staying longer. I will show it to you now and if you let me know, I will reserve it for you to transfer."

She opened the door to this other room which was just down the corridor on the opposite side and I walked in. It was much of the same atmosphere as my room but larger and with two windows both facing the sea. There were two large potted shrubs and the old weathered desk which Maya had mentioned, which I looked past to the incredible blue of the Aegean Sea. It also had a larger shower room and with a bath.

"It's wonderful," I said. I could move in here permanently."

She was delighted that she was able to offer me something that was so suitable. "Then I will reserve it for you," she confirmed. "I will have to charge you some extra because we can obviously get more money for this room, particularly in the summer," she added with an apologetic tone, "But we will talk because if you are staying longer, I will make you a special deal."

"As you have with my present room and I'm very grateful. Thank you Maya!"

"The people in here at the moment kindly agreed that I could show you the room," said she as we returned to the corridor re-locking the room behind us. "Downstairs there is food of some sort served all day. Either go to the bar or find a table and we will come to you."

"I can't understand the backboards," I told her with a smile.

"Just talk to the staff. Most of them speak some English – some better than others. They will explain and will do anything you want within reason and any food or drinks we charge to your room – it's easier." And then before descending the stairs she said, "You are very welcome here Matt– we are pleased to have you. You will be well looked after and for anything at all you just have to ask," she added and held out her hand again. She was genuine and charming.

I unpacked and settled into my room, relaxing on the bed for a while before going down for dinner. I reflected on the suddenness of my departure, the journey itself and the simplicity of my room as I gave thought to my new schedule. In the space of a day, I had a new abode in a faraway place in the sun and a new lifestyle. It was very different to my life and work in London and although feeling strange, it was a nice strange, and exciting. I was looking forward to living the dream.

Downstairs I found a small table by the window and was shortly visited by Maria, the lady I had spoken to on arrival. She gave me a little menu sheet which I hadn't expected, setting out a few of the standard dishes that were on offer and explained, as I understood it, many combinations and possibilities. Her English was passable with patience.

I had red mullet which was fried and served crispy and smoky with vegetables and the ubiquitous Greek chips. There was some chunky homemade bread put on the table with a few separate pots of dips and appetisers. The food was really delicious and plentiful and all washed down with a glass of the unpretentious white house wine poured from a communal bottle. The taverna was filling up with mainly indigenous people it seemed and with very low lighting from an assortment of wall and table lamps and some candles in jars on many of the tables the atmosphere was warm, relaxing and easy-going. From an area by the bar that I couldn't quite see came the sound of a solitary mandolin being played and one couple were dancing together slowly to the music.

Maya came in and walked around as if checking that things were to her liking and she came to me.

"Matt, good evening. Was everything ok for you?"

"Yes thank you. It was excellent and this," I said looking around and gesturing with my hand is lovely. I feel relaxed and quite at home."

"I am very pleased. I hope it doesn't get too noisy for you later. Sometimes we get extra musicians come and people dance."

"That would be lovely to see. Do you ever get problems?" I asked, "being relatively isolated and open to all."

"Greek people may be noisy at times but they don't cause trouble. If there is any trouble it would generally be from tourists but it is rare and doesn't get out of hand. Particularly with him in here," she said as she looked over to the far side of the room.

I followed her gaze to a lone man sitting at a table by the wall. I saw a man probably in his thirties, slim but very well built, looking very fit and strong, eating his food nonchalantly. He was leaning over his food using just a fork in his right hand and his left elbow was on the table. He had long dark hair to his shoulders, gathered around his head by a band tied at the back with the tails hanging down and was wearing a loose shirt with baggy trousers, the sort that trendy artists may wear, and sandals. He was very attractive in an arty sort of way and looked laid back in the extreme. He was serene to the point of almost being in a meditative state. He looked very Greek and reminded one of perhaps a biblical character or a manifestation of an ancient Greek God.

"Is he your bouncer?" I asked.

She gave me a broad smile. "No, but he is a martial arts expert, a black belt I think. Sometimes when you are out walking maybe on the cliff or the beach you may be lucky enough to see him working out. He is amazing! Amazing!" she emphasised. "Sometimes I have watched."

"Is he local?"

"He has a small farm out of the village towards the mountains and he keeps goats – a small herd. His is Stefanos. He's quite solitary, keeps himself to himself, a lovely peaceful man and very well liked. He's a regular here – we're pleased to see him and his English is good if you get into conversation. Not a bouncer as you say but could be very useful if there was trouble." She smiled warmly bowed her head slightly and turned away, leaving me to my thoughts and the prospect of an early night.

Chapter 5

"Good morning Matt," said Maya as I walked into the taverna for breakfast, the first day of my new life.

"Good morning. I'll take this any day to the hustle of London and the morning rush hour," I replied, gesturing with my hands and my eyes around me.

"What can I get you?" she asked when I was seated.

"Are you on duty yourself today?"

"No but I serve you," she said with a smile

"Black coffee and some toast and marmalade, please."

She nodded and put her finger up as if to say 'leave it to me.'

As she turned away, I caught sight of a woman having breakfast who was very different to the average clientele. She looked to be either English or American and as I saw her our eyes met and she acknowledged me with a polite reserved smile. Was it Jennifer? I didn't think so. There was no immediate recognition on my part. The obvious difference was the hair. The Jennifer I had seen on both occasions had long hair – a similar blonde colour but tied and hanging beyond her shoulders. This lady had thick hair but it was short. It was geometrically cut quite sharply into the back of her neck giving an altogether more severe look – a totally different image. Whereas the Jennifer that I had seen gave a relaxed very feminine look, this lady gave a chic lady about town look – smart and purposeful. I studied her profile in a series of brief glimpses being careful not to be seen looking – eye contact for a second time in such a short space of time might seem untoward.

Both times I had seen her previously were at distance – across the road, so I had an overall profile rather than memorable features. The head and shoulders portrait on her website was full frontal which was a view I didn't have at this moment. With different hair, different clothes and from a different angle I couldn't say one way or the other.

On the other hand, according to Alex, she was staying here the same as me and in the short time I had been here she was the only person who, even with imagination, could possibly fit the bill so I wouldn't bet against it. All I could say was that she was not immediately recognisable.

Maya herself brought me my breakfast and it looked lovely. Bread from the village, baked that morning she informed and it was broken into various pieces and toasted. There was a stone pot of locally made orange preserve, a similar stone pot of Greek yoghurt and a large pot of black coffee. The aromas coming from the tray were amazing. It was all vibrant and fresh.

The prices in the taverna were generally so cheap, I didn't really consider it necessary to check them. Whatever items being added to my bill were so very reasonable it wasn't an issue. I'm sure the same items would be more costly in or nearer the big cities but still a fraction of the cost in the UK generally and particularly in London.

"Was that ok for you?" asked Maya, seeing I had finished.

"That was so good. Thank you"

"Have you planned your day?"

"Loosely," I replied. "I'm going to make an initial exploration locally – the little harbour, which looks lovely, and I will walk along the beach. I'm looking forward to that – the views, the sea, the air and the sand under my bare feet and I will enjoy a swim at some point."

"Lovely. You can walk a long way along the beach from here – a very long way! If you walk far enough you will come to series of coves but they are all accessible on foot from the beach. I doubt you'll see a living soul. Would you like the kitchen to pack you a small lunch in a box? Then you can eat when you are ready and you won't have to worry about finding somewhere in such remote surroundings."

"That sounds lovely, Maya! Thank you, I'll pick it up on my way out."

"Enjoy your day and I look forward to seeing you tonight. If you are in," she added before turning away.

I went to my room to get my bag with my board shorts, towel and my writing folder which is always with me on my jaunts to record any thoughts or feelings spontaneously as they arise and even some script if inspiration comes.

Coming back down the stairs, as I approached the doors to the taverna, they suddenly opened without warning – there was no glass in the doors to see through– and the Jennifer possibility and I were staring each other in the face.

"Oh hello!" she said as an involuntary startled reaction.

"Hi," I said with a smile, relieving her embarrassment at nearly knocking me out.

"I... I understand we are both long termers," said she, making introductory conversation.

"Is that similar to a life sentence?" I asked.

She laughed. "Not in a place like this. It's about as near as we can get to paradise isn't it?"

"Absolutely! – from my first impressions."

"I'm Jennifer," she informed, extending her hand.

"Matt," I replied, taking her hand warmly.

So yes, she was indeed Jennifer! Not as I remembered her exactly but very attractive and very personable – charming in fact and her voice was cultured. Her face was quite beautiful with the maturity of her years – some forty six according to Alex. She was lightly made up and with her hair as I now saw it and her disposition, she looked very much like a lady about town and with a purpose. She wasn't laid back as a holiday maker might be and seemed too focused for the average tourist and as she was on her own, she was within her own being, giving a greater authority to her presence. She was wearing a light coloured blouse with a feint blue stripe with the collar up and the sleeves rolled up above the wrists. Her trousers were cream, close around the loins but looser on the legs and she was in cream leather espadrilles. She oozed designer labels. My overall impression was of maybe a city magazine editor on the Mediterranean researching a project but I now had confirmation of the project as I knew it.

"I'm renovating a villa," she informed. "There's so much work to do before it even becomes habitable so I'm staying here in the meantime."

"Oh wonderful. Is it to be a holiday villa, a retreat, or a permanent residence?"

She smiled curiously. "That's an interesting one. I'll certainly be spending a lot of time there. How about you? Are you considering buying a place or are you just here for a limited period?"

35

"I'm looking to start a new life. The Mediterranean beckoned and Greece in particular. I want to write and this seems an ideal escape from the confines of London and city life. Yes, if I settle I will look to buy something."

"Well you've certainly picked an amazing area and this place," she said looking about her, "is a rare find. It's a little gem."

"I'm just going out to get a feel of the area for my first day and for me a long walk along a beach of the Aegean and a possible swim in utter peace is a good start."

"Wonderful! Don't let me hold you up. I'm sure our paths will cross frequently. Nice to talk to you."

"And you," I said warmly before walking through the doors to the bar and awaiting my packed lunch.

So Alex, I thought, the first part of your interesting scenario has come about as planned. 'You're bound to bump into one another' was his prediction and fate had lost no time in bringing it about. 'Bump into' was the operative phrase – she nearly knocked me out with the door.

But why such a change in Jennifer's appearance? The first obvious explanation would be that she has cut her hair, being more suitable for a prolonged stay in a hot climate. And whilst that may be part of it, I sensed there may be more. She could have cut her hair to make it more suited but kept basically to the same image. But this was so different I sensed that a change of image could well have been the prime motive – that maybe the change of look corresponded to a change of outlook, of personality even. She had bought a villa in Greece with a view to living here which even if it was in a semi-permanent way would be a totally different lifestyle and maybe her change of appearance fitted the person she had or wished to become. The old and the new – a life away from Alex?

I put my lunch in my bag and left the taverna, the smell of hot bread and coffee gradually giving way to the scent and atmosphere of the emerging day. The sun was still rising – the heat of the day not yet formed. I took a deep breath taking in the whole of my new experience and filling me with a freshness like no other. I surveyed the vista. I saw the village stretching up to the mountains and to my right the sand edging the intense blue of the Aegean Sea and the small harbour. Small sea birds gave life to it, some perched on the fishing boats others soaring on the gentle breeze that came from the sea wafting its freshness and enlivening the fragrance of the shrubs in bloom. Crystal clear air made for vibrant colours and any discernible sounds had to be detected – they were not apparent. It was the sound of silence.

There was a sleepiness about the place. No-one was hurried. It was as if everything happened by chance rather than design - laid back would be an understatement. How different to city life and the ordered lifestyle in general of the western world. There was no traffic, just the occasional vehicle here and there, no commuters and no school run. People ambled, rarely at pace. To the outsider, there lacked purpose, any intentions were known only to the locals. As the sea lapped against the shore, having little if any tidal influence, so the people led their lives with seemingly little impetus. Humming with the absence of purpose, it was relaxing in the extreme, the atmosphere like a balm. Beauty was apparent in the unseen.

The village looked enticing but I was resolute in my plan to explore the coastline today. To savour the remoteness and the beauty and to swim in the sea – it had been so long.

I made for the shoreline, took off my sandals to walk barefoot on the sand giving me a grounding, a greater connection to what I saw and felt and as I progressed, leaving the village and the harbour far behind, my senses were filled with new experience. The gentle walking, as walking always does, generated thoughts but these were sensual thoughts – not of everyday matter. My routine had gone and I was alone and it was my senses that were exercised feeding my soul. Now I was interacting with the subtleties of this world rather than the harsh realities or forced routine and with the warm sunshine, a place I had longed to be for so long.

After about an hour, I came to a cove and I could see others ahead just as Maya had told me. Seeing an empty cove was a sudden jolt to my senses. There is the initial awe of ostensibly peeping round a corner and discovering a secret – but it was more. A walk along a seemingly never ending shoreline stretching into the distance with a total absence of people is in itself lonely but at every moment you are progressing towards a goal – something ahead. The cove was at once a place of arrival and any loneliness that I had been feeling was now compounded. Rather than a continuance of my walk, it presented as a cauldron of emptiness. Cutting back into the cliff, it was a place in itself and not part of the open shoreline.

I walked to its centre and paused. I turned round taking in everything – the astounding beauty of it all and the solitude as if I had been teleported to an uninhabited world. I felt utterly alone. I contemplated the emptiness and the silence, allowing it all to flow through me before walking on.

On reaching the next cove, I had to turn partly into it as the sea came in further at this point and as I did so I was immediately startled. Suddenly I was not alone. At the back of the cove there was a woman, naked, drying herself with a towel. The shoreline turning in made this a much smaller cave both in depth and width so although the lady was by the cliff itself she was only some twenty meters away from me. From my momentarily sighting of her, she had longish black hair and was evenly suntanned all over. I felt intrusive even though the encounter was completely natural. We both had every right to be where we were and to be doing what we were doing but this lady obviously had the expectation of being alone. I didn't want to intrude on her solitude or even cause her to feel compromised. She had seen me as I had her but I kept on walking without hesitation and not looking towards her again after my initial sighting. She had seemed relaxed about our surprise encounter and gave me a very brief tight mouthed smile as a friendly but terse acknowledgement seeing another being and I simply did the same but I did raise my hand momentarily as if to say 'hi' but without further eye contact.

As I passed the cove and the next one I came across another smaller one where the cliff was not so far from the sea and I decided to make this my destination for lunch. I would have my swim before eating so having set out my pitch by some rocks near the cliff face, I changed into my board shorts. And my immediate thought was why am I doing this? It was so remote and swimwear would appear to be optional. But I had no impulse in that regard. Yes, I have done so in Cornwall in quiet private moments and occasionally for a moonlight swim but most of my time in the sea is with a surf board or wild swimming in all weathers so my board shorts and even a wet suit and I are pretty synonymous.

After a wonderfully relaxing time in the cool water, I returned to my belongings and sitting on a rock, enjoyed the simple lunch the kitchen had packed for me. Afterwards l laid out on my towel to relax and sunbathe and for this I *was* in a state to get an all over tan. I was refreshed and at total peace. I simply allowed my mind to drift, awash with my senses in tune with the atmosphere that was about me in my solitude. I lost track of time but when seeing the sun much lower in the sky and realising I would soon be screened by the cliffs behind me, I packed my things and made the long walk back.

As I approached the taverna, I could see a Harley Davidson motorcycle parked not in the parking area but more to the front, just away from some of the outside chairs and tables. I've always had a feeling for these bikes and this one was a beauty. It was very much of the easy rider configuration with the high shaped handlebars and the low saddle which was elongated to take a pillion passenger. The main frame was black as was the petrol tank – the paint job exceptional with the Harley badge on it highlighted. The rest of the bike was stainless steel and chrome including the front forks and it all looked stunning.

As I took a closer look, a voice came from behind me, "You like my bike?"

I started to turn but Stefanos appeared alongside. "Is this yours? I *love* your bike."

"Thanks man," was his response, in true hippy fashion. He was as I remembered him from when Maya pointed him out in the taverna the previous evening but he was now in conversation, not a more distant figure and his voice matched his image – laid back but with an immediate sincerity. Whilst his looks were classic Greek, his English had an accent more international in its pronunciation, suggestive that he had spent time overseas. His presence was amazing.

"I think it looks stunning. Is it a hybrid?"

"I don't know its history. It had been in a crash and a guy I know bought it for renovation. The forks are new and it's had quite a bit of work done on it. We think it's at least twenty years old. Do you ride?"

"I have done but not on a bike like this. I had a smaller standard bike for running around in my early university days and I loved it but I couldn't carry a surf board on it so it had to go and I've had a car of some sort since."

"You surf?" said Stefanos enthused.

"Yes it was a passion when I was able but when I moved to London it was too far away."

"I surf, man."

"But you can't surf in Greece, surely?"

"Yes. It's possible. In Greece, we have the Meltemi winds. They blow from the north over the Aegean on and off through the summer. The seas are not like the world's main surfing areas but sometimes they can be good."

"Near here?"

"Yeah, man. Not too far south from here the land curves out to sea quite a bit and with a good northerly wind the waves can be good. But with less wind I kite surf – it's ideal for that. Have you kite surfed?"

"No. No I haven't. That's something I've always wanted to try. That's extreme sport."

"So's surfing in a heavy sea, man. You're staying here aren't you?"

"Yes long term."

"Come with me. When the winds are right I could let you know."

"You know, I'd like that. I'll look forward to it."

"You're welcome – you love my bike, man," he said with the broadest of smiles. I'm Stefanos," he added, raising his hand.

"Matt," I acknowledged raising my hand to his for a high five and we both smiled in appreciation as he straddled his bike and put on his helmet.

I walked towards the door of the taverna and as I did so, I saw Jennifer sitting at a table under a tree nearby. Seeing me she raised a hand and smiling, called out "Have you had a good day? How's the Aegean?"

I walked to her. "I've had solitude, peace and beauty and the Aegean gave me a refreshing swim. Have you been working on your villa?"

"Planning. No toil today," said Jennifer and as she did so Stefanos started his motorcycle, giving that unique signature tick-over sound of a Harley Davidson, reportedly sounding like: potato-potato-potato. And as he pulled away there was just a gentle evocative hum from its V-twin engine. There was no harsh acceleration of a showy take-off – he was no biker from hell! I sensed this was a gentle man with a lifestyle as beautiful as his mind.

"Ah that lovely ripple of sound can only come from a Harley," I said."

Jennifer smiled. "You've met Stefanos I see."

"Yes, we've just had a chat. He's a fellow surfer he tells me."

"*You* surf? Oh he's passionate. You'll have more than a shared interest there."

"I was surprised to hear there's surfing in Greece."

"Yes, I was surprised and not too far from here when the wind's right."

"He seems really nice."

"He's lovely. He's helping me with the villa. He's brilliant with wood."

"Really?"

"He's very artistic generally – got a good feel for spaces and the aesthetics and he's worked with the woodworkers, the craftsmen, in the Far East. He's very talented."

"So carving?"

"Carving, panelling with a flair, apart from general woodwork and he has a great appreciation of the architecture here. I have a builder for the main structural work but Stefanos does most of the visible woodwork. He's a wizard!"

"He sounds amazing."

She smiled and nodded, her lips closed and I sensed an affinity between them which was bound to be a positive factor in the renovation project. I hadn't seen where Stefanos came from just now but there was an empty glass on the table apart from Jennifer's so I presumed they had just sat together, conferring.

"I think you've found a friend," said Jennifer. "I'm pleased for both of you. Are you eating here tonight? It's going to be hectic. There's some sort of celebration on. Music, dancing – busy, busy."

41

"Oh thanks for the warning." I put my hand up in acknowledgement and turned to continue to my room.

As I was getting ready for the evening, my phone rang. Maya explained that it was a special evening with music and dancing and they were very busy with all tables being taken. But she had reserved two for me one inside, the other outside – if I wanted to eat it was my choice.

"Outside would be lovely," I told her. "How thoughtful of you, thank you so much."

"You're very welcome," said she. "The table is under a tree with a reserved sign on it."

As I went down the stairs for my meal I could hear music and the burble of a crowd in the taverna and as I entered, I had to weave my way around musicians, people dancing and people drinking or just chatting. The place was full and I welcomed the less hectic atmosphere of the outside area as I found my table. I was to enjoy my food and a drink under a tree with the strains of very Greek music and the gaiety seeping into the balmy night air, with various lanterns and low lights making it atmospheric. I reflected on the day's exploration and planned tomorrow, quite enjoying the ethnic mayhem but glad I was on the fringe of it.

Chapter 6

I had decided to explore the coastline further up beyond where I had been. I would drive along the cliffs which would give me a bird's eye view and then circle back inland, seeing some of the mountain villages. With a map, I planned my route over breakfast in the taverna and when returning to my room I had a surprise.

I went through the doors to the stairs and was immediately in the company of an air hostess – obviously so by her uniform. We made eye contact on meeting and I simply said "Hi," as an acknowledgement as I passed her and started up the stairs. Reaching the halfway landing I paused to look back at her.

She was stunning. A dark blue tight skirt to the knees with high heels a short sleeved white fitted blouse with an insignia and a coloured silk scarf around her neck in the open collar. Her long black hair was tied back in a ponytail and she had very dark brown eyes. She was obviously Greek by her features, expertly made up and slim with a superb figure. Her body and the uniform were made for each other. If I saw her in the first class lounge at London Airport I would be guilty of a few double takes but seeing her here in a taverna in remote Greece, I was stunned.

She was bending down doing something with her luggage – a suitcase on wheels and a largish shoulder bag. Her suit jacket was folded and draped over her arm. She was looking up as I looked down so we made eye contact again. She smiled a reserved smile but seemed hesitant.

"Are you ok?" I asked. "Can I help?"

"No. I'm fine but thank you," she replied in a deep seemingly cultured voice, her English pronunciation excellent with just a hint of an alluring accent. She then opened the doors and walked through towing her suitcase on its wheels, her jacket still over her arm. Hoping for another sighting, I hurried to my room and across to the window which looks over the front of the taverna and there she was, walking to a waiting minibus. And oh! That walk – elegant, purposeful and characteristic. She had a gait that added almost eroticism to her movement and certainly intrigue. I watched her chat briefly to the driver before climbing on board.

I'd put her in her early thirties maybe, possibly a year or two younger than me, but there was an obvious maturity about her and she was completely natural, nothing seemed contrived. She was sheer class. I was totally captivated.

She had certainly stayed at the taverna en-route. But en-route where? There were no major airports nearby, certainly none that would be used by the big airlines that I know of and if she was on holiday, why would she be in uniform for her return with so far to travel?

However great my pleasure was at seeing her, it was balanced by my disappointment that she was leaving and not arriving. I was denied the pleasure of meeting her during my stay. So near yet so far! I wasn't sure whether it would be a treasured memory, positively enhancing my imagination, or whether it might induce discontent, compounding my loneliness.

One question in my mind was answered. If it was between her and Jennifer, lovely as Jennifer was, I didn't feel an urge towards her such that I did with the Greek air hostess I had just seen. And that was beyond the uniform – it was her whole being. Call it intuition or gut feeling, it was that form of inner knowing that is beyond our understanding.

I drove out of the village taking the coastal road and I got a loftier view, a different perspective of the coast and the Aegean than when I was walking along the beach where I was part of it. After a few miles, as the road turned nearer the cliff edge, I could see the series of coves, the first few of which, were my destination when walking previously. I was aiming for an area that Maya had shown me on the map which was much further on. It was a small headland surrounded by a series of rocky inlets which according to her was very beautiful and very isolated and with so many individual little areas was popular with those in the know who wanted solitude. Following the map, I took a smaller road that was not much more than a track as it progressed and I went as far as it would take me and then parked and took a vague path to the headland.

The view was breath-taking. The deep blue of the Aegean meeting the softer blue of the sky and below me the little headland surrounded by numerous tiny sandy coves formed by what looked like rock falls. I started to descend one of the several tracks that would go down to the shoreline and suddenly became aware of a distant figure swimming in the sea. I descended further, not knowing which cove I would be taken to and not by design I got a closer view of the swimmer, no longer swimming but walking back to the rocks in his little cove. Even from my distance I could see he was naked and as he continued, I recognised him. It was Stefanos! After my surprise of recognising him, my first thought was would I see him working out. Having been told that he frequently does so here on the shoreline, surely he would take the opportunity of his solitude to do so and I would dearly like to see that. He disappeared from view nearing the cliff so I descended further and further hoping to get a view if he was indeed going to work out. I didn't sight him anymore and I eventually arrived at a private little cove at sea level and fortunately not the one he was using – I wouldn't intrude on his privacy. I had hoped to get a view before I got down to sea level but that didn't happen. I sat down on some rocks to rest, resigned that I wouldn't now see any more of him. Time had moved on since my sighting and he may even have been on his way back up.

Then I became aware of movement through small gaps in the rocks and sensed it may be Stefanos in the adjacent little cove. With my shoes off I gingerly crept over the sand to the rocks to see if it was him. I really didn't want to intrude so I was careful not to create observable movement on my side. I manoeuvred to see through one of the small gaps and what I saw staggered me beyond belief. I was stunned! It was indeed Stefanos but with him was Jennifer, both naked and they were making love. I hadn't foreseen that. I hadn't remotely considered them in a relationship. They were having sex and not lying down on their towels but standing, with Jennifer leaning slightly back against a tall rock just a few meters from me. They were well and truly in the act, facing each other, he by his slow rhythmic movement pressing her against the rock intermittently and with a free hand exciting her breasts, she with one hand on his shoulder and the other in his hair at the back of his neck. The expression on their faces spoke volumes. It was intense. It wasn't hurried at all. It was rhythmic, sensual, artistic – poetry in motion. I was over-

45

awed, initially at the shock of seeing them together sexually, but it was the apparent disparate pairing that was visually highly erotic. He, the younger virile Adonis, a character, not a stereotype of the modern world, his hair wild, his body toned, a semi hippy martial artist and she, the mature sophisticated lady about town with her short hair cut geometrically into the back of her neck. The thought alone of such a pairing would in itself be erotic but seeing it so graphically and at short range and in motion was stunning. It was as if it was contrived – an enactment from the Karma Sutra perhaps or an act in an exclusive night club, choreographed for maximum erotic intrigue. I felt heady but at the same time I felt guilty at being a spectator and I started to back away very carefully so as not to disturb them or give them any notion that they were not alone. As I was leaving, I heard Jennifer gasping momentarily, seemingly uncontrollably until it faded to stuttered sighs. As I started to ascend a path back up to the clifftop, I looked around occasionally making sure that I could not be seen as I got higher but they were too close to the cliff for them to see up and I was so relieved to have left without being seen.

Back in my car I headed inland continuing to climb and coming upon a little taverna in a small mountain village I pulled in and decided to have some lunch. I sat at an outside table and would enjoy a slice of their pizza with a small beer under the shade of a parasol and I continued to reflect on what I had seen and as I did so, my mind's eye was creative in its vision. Jennifer's cries became ever louder, drifting with the gentle breeze that enveloped their nakedness and had I have stayed, I would have seen Jennifer's legs buckle with Stefanos supporting her. Haunting – the sound of someone's most private moment, rarely, if ever to be heard. It was a crescendo, the final movement to a beautiful symphony and with the whole event being amplified in my mind, I questioned how much of it I had seen and how much of it I had conjured as a continuation as I walked away. The two were intertwined and inseparable. Maybe I had lingered longer than I remembered.

And I thought of Alex. His assertion that he didn't think sex was a priority for Jennifer and his curiosity as to would she or wouldn't she, with me being head hunted to find out. Well I'm sorry Alex, whatever might or might not have been in that regard, nature has naturally pre-empted you. In your one lapse into bloke-speak – the club changing room banter – you leaned to me and whispered "She must be due for a service!" You are not to know it but I would say she's had a major service, or as Shakespeare might have put it with more refinement, "The lady hath already been plucked."

I still felt guilty at being an intruder on their privacy. My expectation, if anything, was to see Stefanos working out, not making out, but I couldn't un-see what I had seen. And I didn't want to. As I continued to re-live the moment I felt privileged to have seen it. I felt both guilty and grateful for a natural opportunity of seeing such a pairing for real. It was natural and not in any way obscene or crude and certainly not indecent because they were discrete by their isolation. It was in fact quite beautiful, artistic and the emotions were almost palpable. And I thought of how powerful it must be for them. There must be an element of the attraction of opposites but with a shared love of the beautiful in a creative working environment and in the stunning setting and climate of the Aegean coast.

But it wasn't just the physical act that intrigued me, it was the psychology of the pairing and the situation. Was it purely sexual, of the moment, or was it deeper. I certainly wasn't of the opinion that it was a one off. There was obviously some affection there – maybe they had fallen in love. Maybe it was for the longer term but whatever, what I had seen would remain private to them. It served only to enhance my imagination and would go no further and that imagination was becoming more creative by the day with what I had experienced on my walk the day before and in the absence of an outlet myself, if it was a blessing, it was in disguise.

Driving back, I felt a warm glow. I really did feel privileged to have experienced their joy and I was pleased for them. They had obviously found something meaningful between them and I was still thinking about them as I took my table for my evening meal back at the taverna. In my mind I wished them well.

Chapter 7

"Had a good day?" asked Jennifer as she diverted to my table to have a few words before sitting at hers for her evening meal.

"Yes, yes I have. I drove into the mountains to see some of the villages."

"Oh wonderful!"

"Lunch and a beer outside a little taverna in the mountains in shorts and sandals – it doesn't get much better. And you?"

"Yes, thank you. A day on the beach relaxing. Some days it's just so lovely to be wild and free," she said as she turned for her table.

No sooner had she sat down when I heard the unmistakeable sound of a Harley Davidson pulling up outside and moments later Stefanos came in. He went to Jennifer's table put down his things and then seeing me he came over. I was hoping he hadn't seen me earlier and that his coming to me had a different purpose.

"Hi man. The wind's going to pick up over the next few days so I'm hoping to get some surfing in. Are you up for it?"

"Sure thing!"

"Great. Can we get our phone numbers? I'll ring you."

We entered our numbers, he raised his hand for a high five and with the smile of a friend he re-joined Jennifer.

It's the first time I've seen them together and I wondered whether it was generally known that they were an item or were having a relationship over and above a working one. Dinner in the evening is generally seen as more intimate than being together during the day. But I suspected that both Jennifer and Stefanos wouldn't concern themselves. I think both they and the Greek people would accept it for what it is and not bat an eyelid. I didn't sense that gossip would be on the agenda – the romantic nature of the Greek personality combining with the climate they would simply accept whatever they see as everyday life without question. Very different to social life in the UK.

Having enjoyed my meal, I walked to the bar for a drink and to listen to the musician. There was a guy in the corner at the end of the bar playing a mandolin. I had heard him previously when eating but he wasn't visible - it was simply background music. Here by the bar I was able to see him and it gave him a presence – I felt part of it. It was gentle, melodic and atmospheric which was very different to the previous night's mayhem.

As I approached the bar I saw a very attractive lady at the end, talking to Maria who usually served me. This new lady smiled warmly and walked along to meet me. I'd not seen her before but she could certainly be added to the collection of highly attractive women who seemed to frequent this place.

Black long hair hanging freely below her shoulders wearing a loose soft blouse with baggy sleeves hanging off the shoulders and from what I could see from over the counter, was a longish skirt tight around her loins but loosening into folds below, both of a floral pattern in muted colours. The sound and nature of her walk suggested she was wearing heels of some sort. To me she looked very much traditional Greek but with designer influence.

"What can I get you?" she asked in perfect English in a very affable manner.

"Could I have a brandy please?" she broadened her smile and walked along to the spirits to show me what they had. They were not inverted into bar optics but were in bottles with pouring measures and a selection of spirit measuring cups around them on a table. She put out her hand towards them and was about to speak when I enquired. "Courvoisier?"

"I'm sorry, we don't have French," she informed with a hint of her eyes rolling round but apologetically nevertheless. She picked up two bottles and two small shot glasses and put them on the counter in front of me. "We have Greek brandy," she explained. This is the traditional one and this is the local one," said she identifying the bottles. Her English really was excellent – I could be talking to someone in London rather than in a remote Greek taverna. She had a deep voice with just a trace of an accent. "Try them," she added as she poured just a little of each into the shot glasses. "This one is very popular here – we sell much more of that," she said pointing to the local one. "It is a third of the price of what a French one would be and that," she said pointing to the other is half the price.

"That's very genuine of you," I acknowledged, "recommending one that makes less revenue for you."

"Oh, no, we make more on the local one than the others."

I couldn't resist! "So basically, you're offering me two to three times as much of what I didn't ask for, for the same price as what I did ask for and you make more money out of it," I said with the broadest of smiles. "Did you have to go on a course for that?" Did she laugh! She found that highly amusing. She laughed and laughed in that deep tone and as I looked into her face my mind imagined her hair tied back in a ponytail and the penny was dropping. Could she and the air hostess be one and the same? Her eyes were more heavily made up and she gave a totally different image but that deep voice and above all her presence were compelling. It had to be her, surely.

"Did we meet briefly earlier today?" I asked.

Her smile broadened. "Yes, I think we did – briefly."

"As an air hostess."

"Yes."

"So either you had one of the shortest flights in history or you were going to a fancy dress party."

She laughed again, keeping her lips closed which was endearing before saying, "I was going to a photo shoot in the mountains. You know, come fly with me is the caption with me on the mountain top, my arms outstretched enticingly and my scarf blowing in the wind," and she then demonstrated the pose – da, dah… "I am presently the face of the airline."

"And you really are an air hostess?"

"Yes."

"And you work here occasionally?"

"I live here."

"You live here?"

"Maya is my mother. Elena costopolou," she said, extending her hand.

I was astounded but deeply enthused. "Matt Rochester," I said, taking her hand lightly.

"I know," she informed. Hotshot lawyer from the UK."

"Hotshot lawyers come from America not the UK."

"Not this one."

"So what makes you think I'm hotshot?"

"You look it," said she canting her head slightly and looking into me.

"Maybe if my ability precedes me so obviously, I should increase my fees," I told her.

She laughed, "What do you think to the brandy?"

"Actually, I quite like this one," I said pointing to the local one. The first sip seemed a bit coarse but it's mellowed and it has a lovely musty after taste."

"Yes, it's the most popular here. Greek people like their brandy. I drink it!"

"Right, pour me one of those."

"A double?"

"No, I'll start with a single and if I still find it agreeable I'll have another later. Will you have one? Can I get you one too?"

"Thank you, yes, but I'll have it a bit later. I'm discussing menus at the moment," said she looking towards the kitchen entrance at the end of the bar.

I smiled and nodded. "I'll take mine over there to that table by the wall before it is taken," I told her. "I want to enjoy the music."

I opened my writing folder and started to construct my thoughts in the hope of shaping the beginnings of my novel. It was lovely, the low lights, the candles in jars, the smell of herbs that were growing abundantly in pots all around overlaid occasionally from wafts of food when the kitchen door opened and a meal was brought by me. After a while, my concentration was broken by Elena approaching me with the bottle of brandy in her hand, seeing my glass was empty.

"Will you have the second half of the double?" she asked amusingly.

"Yes I will thank you," I said with enthusiasm, "I really enjoyed that." And as she poured it I asked, "Will you have yours now?" whereupon she promptly brought her left hand from behind her back and put an empty glass on the table opposite mine as she laughed. I gestured for her to sit opposite me and she did so, hardly waiting to be asked and poured hers, leaving the bottle on the table. She looked into my face and again gave me that endearing smile with her lips closed but now she was very close, the round tables being quite small. Her presence was enormous and I felt privileged.

51

"So if you're working on the menus could that mean that there might be one I can understand?" I asked her. She had a quizzical smile. "I can't understand the blackboards on the wall, they mean nothing to me."

"Nobody can understand the blackboards on the wall," I was told. "They are written by people who can't write for people who mostly can't read, the chalk is heavily smudged and they're out of date anyway."

"They look good."

"That's it! They're decoration basically."

"Sorry if I'm taking things too seriously."

"Oh no, you must. They're there to be taken seriously. The fact that they're virtually meaningless is not the issue. They set the scene – they're what people expect to see." Most people who look at them get the gist of it and then order what they had in mind when they came in." She was delightful. Amusing and self-deprecating. "I understand you have come here to write," she said. And then touching my leather folder she asked, "Is it working for you?"

"I think it will. Early days but I find it very creative here as I hoped I would."

"So – a novel?"

"Yes. I would like to write with a philosophical content and for starters was going to chart my reasons for my proposed life change and how it pans out. I have a publisher who knows me well and suggested I write it as a novel. Possibly loosely based on real events but with changed names obviously."

"To protect the innocent," said Elena smiling.

"Something like that."

"Do you have a title? Some writers have a title at the outset and that forms the catalyst for the story rather than developing a title as it is written."

I put my hands together and with my arms partly on the table, I leaned slightly to her to engage more deeply. "That's quite profound. No. No title as yet but it will come. I must say your English is really excellent – not just your pronunciation but your vocabulary and your phrasing."

"I studied at university in England."

"What did you study?"

"English," she said laughing. I did a BA Hons degree – English language and literature and some classics."

I too laughed. "Brilliant," I told her and pushing my writing folder slightly towards her suggested, "perhaps you should do it for me or at least start me off."

"I think you are very capable but perhaps I could be your muse?" She really was lovely.

"What a good idea!" our eyes were meeting more frequently and our voices softened. We had an instant rapport. The conversation was easy going, meaningful and fun. Her last sentence seemed to imply that we would enjoy a friendship and I felt inwardly emotional that this amazing and unusual person that I had just met was seemingly to be part of my life here in Greece. Maybe I wasn't to be so lonely.

"So – why an air hostess?" I asked her.

"I was going to teach, but nearing the end of my university time, I met a Greek girl at a party, who was an air hostess for a major Greek airline and we got talking. She told me her airline would welcome someone like me. 'Why not consider it for a year or two – see the world, both geographically and by interaction, before settling down?' she suggested. 'Like a very immersive gap year or two.' Shortly after, I got a phone call from the airline which was followed by a meeting. That was," – she pursed her lips and closed one eye, – "that was seven years ago."

"You obviously love it."

"Yes. The airline have promoted me several times. I am now more involved in training, and supervision. They sometimes use me for prestigious flights and for some charter flights on the smaller aircraft, it's quite varied. I still get the buzz when boarding and every time this huge machine accelerates down the runway and the surge when it takes off. It's adventure and I'm in charge of the safety and wellbeing. I feel both humble and proud."

As I looked into her I saw the ingredient of her maturity – a great depth. I thought the airline very fortunate. They had more than her physical presence but I think they would have seen that possibility from the outset.

She brought the conversation back to the topical. "Have you seen much of your new surroundings yet?"

"The coastline, both on foot along the beach and by car further along the cliff and some mountain villages."

"This village?"

"Not yet."

She looked thoughtful and was somewhat hesitant before speaking. "Tomorrow… tomorrow I am going to the church briefly and then the village. Would you like to come with me? I could show you around and maybe introduce you here and there. But do say if you have other plans."

My heart missed a beat. I recalled my thoughts when I first saw her in her uniform earlier and was aware of my feelings now. I could hardly believe what was happening. "I'd like that very much, Elena. Thank you! What time?"

"Nine… ten, it doesn't matter. I'll see you at breakfast."

A day of wonderful sightseeing, an astounding revelation and the promise of a dream coming true. I would sleep well!

Chapter 8

My usual breakfast was pleasantly interrupted by firm approaching footsteps and the appearance of a highly attractive lady – instantly recognisable Elena but her appearance was different yet again. Outwardly she presented differently to the Elena I had met twice before.

The same loose black hair but her make-up was different, particularly around the eyes. She was wearing a loose fitting white blouse with tight fitting denim jeans and black leather boots with a fairly high heel. Instead of a belt, she wore a wide black cloth band around her waist, more like a cumber band, lapping partly over her blouse. To me, her dress was very Greek, complimenting her features. She seemed to change her appearance to suit the occasion and with her make-up, quite dramatically so. In effect I had seen three different Elenas each with their own personality.

"Hi Matt," she said as I stood up and gestured to the spare chair at my table which she pulled out and sat down. As soon as she was seated, a lady brought a tray with a large jug of coffee, some cream and a type of pastry. "There's plenty of coffee here but is there anything else you would like," she asked.

"No I'm fine, thanks Elena." She spoke a few words of Greek to the lady and we were on our own facing each other.

"What is that?" I asked looking at her pastry.

"Bougatsa," she told me. "Several layers of filo pastry filled with semolina custard, chocolate and cinnamon. Very traditional Greek sweet pastry. Try some."

"I've had my toasted bread," I told her.

"I insist!" She cut off a small section and put it on my plate with a little of the cream. The rest of the cream went on her pastry and in her coffee. "You will be leaving this taverna having tried bougatsa," she told me.

"That's really nice. I like the pastry and the cinnamon is quite strong."

"The pastry is very important – we make our own filo here."

We chatted away over our coffees with the same rapport that we had the previous evening. We shared thoughts and had fun and it was spontaneous as before. I so enjoyed her company and was looking forward to our walk into the village.

Breakfast finished, we set off. As we left the taverna I became immediately aware of her walk. I had seen it previously as I had watched her from my window, walking to her transport in her uniform. I saw it as most unusual and characteristic then but walking alongside her it was involving – her presence in motion. She was shorter than me and taking probably two steps to my one. They were determined steps, each one pushed forward and put to the ground resolutely with her body movement rhythmical – characteristic and strangely elegant.

"I'll show you the church. Will you come in with me?"

"Yes, I'd like that."

"It's small and very old – over a thousand years supposedly."

"Really? That sounds amazing. I'd love to experience it."

Are you religious Matt?"

"My beliefs accord more with the eastern philosophies but a church is still a place of reverence to me. I have respect both for its significance and for your individual devotion."

"Thanks Matt," said she pausing briefly as she smiled and looked into me before pushing open the old wooden door. It was indeed very small and once inside, we were immediately enveloped by a pungent smell – a combination of incense, candle wax and that which is given off by the fabric of an ancient building. The walls were painted with large faded murals of religious figures from the early medieval period, which Elena explained to me as saints of their time. She took a black silk scarf from her shoulder bag and draped it over her hair with the ends loosely around her neck. She then took two small candles from a side table offering one to me and put a few coins in the box.

"Thank you," I said as we lit them from those already burning and set them into the sand box with the others. She then walked to the front, bowed to the table which served as an altar, crossed herself and sat in prayer. I joined her, sitting in meditative peace.

After a while she turned to me and smiled, "Ok?" she asked, "shall we go?"

She took off the scarf as we walked outside returning it to her bag and put on some large dark sunglasses and said, "The head covering is my sign of respect – of humility. It is a place of sanctity. A tiny place of refuge from the realities of this world where I can clear my mind and listen in quietness and solitude."

I was moved. This was a very strong lady. Whilst firmly anchored in her roots, she works in a very different world, literally the 'jet set' and when she returns, she has a small place of refuge where she can give respect to a higher authority to help give her a balance, strength and a sense of purpose.

We strolled through the village, my charming host pointing out places of interest and the local services and introduced me to one or two people as the morning passed. One thing was for sure – Elena was well liked and greatly respected.

Later, as we reached a small taverna at the far end of the village with a number of outside tables, she asked "Would you like a coffee? Maybe some lunch? "

"That sounds nice but are you ok for time?"

"Of course!" said she, looking into my face. We seated ourselves at a table under a parasol and perused the menu. "Will you have something? The food here is good." We were approached by a jovial man who was clearly delighted to see Elena. They spoke in Greek briefly then Elena said "This is Matt from England. He is staying at the taverna. Matt, this is Marin."

"I speak some English," said he, "I try." We exchanged a few words but his English was broken and sometimes difficult to understand but he was charming and seemed pleased to show some ability in a foreign language. We both ordered a small beer and also the Greek salad.

"Marin waits on the tables and his wife Apphia is in the kitchen with a helper. Nice people, popular in the village – they get by."

As Elena took off her sunglasses, I asked her, "So, have you always lived here?"

"Yes, I was born here. My mother trained in hospitality in a large London hotel for some years. She met my father who was a trained chef and the assistant hotel manager. They got married and decided to find a little place of their own back here in Greece. So they bought this place and I was born here but after twelve years my father died. He'd had a nasty head injury in his youth which they say left him with a weakness and he had an aneurysm. He was forty eight. I was just ten years old."

"Ah, I'm so sorry. Was he Greek?"

"Yes, and I loved him. He was my dad." Her eyes were moist and she was visibly emotional.

I put my hand on her arm and kept it there as I said again, "I'm so sorry. How dreadful for you." And then to lighten the mood I said, "So – you're a hundred per cent Greek."

"One hundred and ten per cent actually and like all Greeks, full of passion," I was told.

"Yes, as a race that's inborn isn't it?"

"In everything they do – their art, music and dancing, their food, their relationships – in life itself, their whole being."

"And the men too," I said, inviting a response.

"Tell me about it! From a woman's point of view, whilst it can be flattering, it can also be a pain. A conversation can often lead to an expectation of romance in its most demonstrative form – if you understand me. It can be tiresome," she said, her eyes rolling round with her face giving a war weary expression. "When God gave out testosterone I think maybe the Greek men got more than their fair share." I had to smile.

"I like the way you put that – damning but subtle."

"So you think I'll make a good muse?"

"Bring it on!" We laughed together. "But you love this place – this village, this part of Greece."

"I love this place very much. I love my mother and I love the taverna. I've made my own life with my mother's blessing but these are my roots. I help her whenever I can. She has made me a junior partner in the business and I participate when I'm home."

"Do you cook?"

"Very much so on occasions. That's another passion. I was brought up on it."

"And you Matt. Are you giving up your legal career for a life in the sun?"

"Ostensibly yes but that's a long story."

"I'm in no hurry," said she, canting her head slightly and looking at me with encouragement.

"Where do I begin?" I paused to choose my words. "I wanted to convict the guilty and acquit the innocent but that puts it too simply. It's been said that if you want to find the truth, don't look in a courtroom and to some extent I share that viewpoint. I have an innate sense of justice and fair play. I think it was there as a kid but I became aware of it in my youth. I tried to stop bullies at school and I had to intervene when on the beach, I saw kids destroying other kid's sandcastles when they went for a paddle in the sea and it applied itself more deeply as I got older. People who destroy other people's pleasure – other people's lives. It interested me to study law where that innate sense of justice was given substance. I could make a difference."

"Where did you study law?"

"Oxford."

"Wow!"

"Yes, I loved it and I didn't find it too difficult to be honest. A slog yes but I think having such an interest to digest it helped me to absorb it with relative ease and I loved the debating. I was part of the debating society and at that level with the depth of it, the use of words and phrasing and the lessons learnt were a great joy." Elena seemed transfixed, looking into me. "I did enjoy taking those skills into the courts but I became disappointed and more so as time went on. My determination to expose a truth was often tempered by the very words we were using. It became a game of words, a play on words, a misconstruing of words and often taken out of context. And always subject to rules that often work counter to their intention. I frustrated and not through lack of ability. I found myself winning arguments by going somewhat away from the truth and sometimes, although successful, I hated myself afterwards. I wasn't there to play games and win debates. So I took a more backroom role, contracts and legal advice, which allows me licence to engage deeply without playing games."

"I think I know exactly what you mean," said Elena profoundly.

"I don't knock it too much, the system may have flaws but it's the best we've got. I've had ten years in court and I've helped a lot of people and I'm still able to do some background work online – contracts and opinions."

59

"You obviously got to the stage where you wanted out of court work."

"Mm, but couple that with the fact that I was probably not of the disposition for that world in the first place and you have the perfect storm."

"Oh tell me. Why, Matt?"

"I was better born to a surf board than a courtroom."

"You surf?" asked an enthused Elena.

"Big time!"

"Wow!"

"I surfed as a youth and through my university years. Surfing and wild swimming."

Elena touched my arm again. "Where Matt?"

"The west country mainly – Devon and Cornwall. It was a passion. Virtually no seas were too rough if the waves were right and I would often swim round a headland in heavy seas and walk back over the cliff path. The adrenalin almost went off the scale at times."

She put her elbows on the table with her fists together under her chin and leaned towards me, her face almost into mine. "Tell me more," she said.

"So the point is not that I should actually be surfing rather than in a courtroom but that there is the mechanism within me that could surely be better expressed than being in a courtroom. My soul is elsewhere. Exactly what that elsewhere should have been, I'm not sure but it's come to a head now."

"So a free spirit is going to write in a sunny remote location."

"Nail on the head," I told her.

We paused as our beers and the wonderful fresh salads were brought to us. She poured her beer into a glass and then mine and we started to eat. We chatted away at length, the conversation becoming more general – life in general. I loved talking to her. She was confident and authoritative but in a calm and considered way. Her English was excellent and with her deep voice and subtle accent she had intrigue. She was very attractive. With the salads finished a pot of coffee was brought to us and Elena took out an unusual packet of cigarettes.

"Do you mind?" she asked.

"No, not at all. Please go ahead."

"Would you like one?" she asked as she opened the packet and showed me. They were long and black.

"No but thank you. They look unusual – almost like small cheroots."

"Indonesian. They're a mixture of tobacco and cloves plus some other ingredients. Have a smell," said she putting one under my nose.

"Mm they do smell good. Other ingredients?"

She smiled. "They vary. I enjoy them occasionally. They make me feel good. Are you sure you won't try?"

"I'm tempted but no."

"Have you ever smoked?"

"Yes, in my surfing days I rolled my own but now only occasionally. I can honestly say I've never really been addicted as such but I'm not averse if I feel the urge."

She lit hers, sat back a little from the table and crossed her legs. God she looked amazing! I pictured her in her uniform as I had seen her and imagined her walking down the aisle of the airliner. I could imagine the thoughts of many of the male passengers, young and old, and here was I sitting outside a taverna with her in a remote Greek village, engaging deeply as she relaxed smoking her unusual cigarette, possibly with dubious contents. Her Hellenic features added to her allure and her presence was enormous. But it wasn't just the kudos for me. Yes that was powerful enough but I saw more. I was feeling what I sensed when I first saw her, that there was a factor in her to which I was drawn but couldn't define. Was it wishful thinking or a sixth sense? As I was getting to know her I believed it to be the latter. We were engaging and I knew she was an amazing person and I felt privileged.

She put her head slightly to one side as if in consideration and with a little cigarette smoke visible as she exhaled, she said, "You look like a surfer."

"I thought I looked like a hotshot lawyer."

"You do! When we first spoke I saw you as a hotshot lawyer who could possibly surf but now I see you as a rugged surfer with brains."

I laughed. "Rugged?"

61

"Oh yes. Your hair is longish, your body is toned and ...well, your whole being as I see you now. Did you wear a wig in court?"

"Sometimes. They're generally only worn for criminal cases now. When I did, I tied my hair at the back of my neck."

She smiled and canted her head slightly. "Yes, I can see that," she said. "Mm. A rebel with a cause and your hair tied behind a wig defines my description – a free spirit with brains. That would be one occasion when both of you are visible. I think you are a strong character to remain true to both causes."

"I don't know how I see *you* overall. I'm intrigued. The first time I saw you, you were the quintessential international air hostess albeit with Greek features, groomed to perfection with your hair in a ponytail. The second time you were made up and dressed differently with your hair loose about you, very much Greek and casually authoritative in the taverna and today I see you as the lady about town, sophisticated but in a bohemian way. The only common thread is that you look amazing in each of your modes."

She smiled. "Thank you Matt and what about the first time you saw me?"

"I've said. Amazing in your uniform."

"No, I said the first time you saw me."

The penny dropped for a second time. "That was you in the cove?"

"Yes! That was me nude in the cove. Did you see me as amazing on that occasion too?" I was stunned into silence. "Is hotshot lawyer from the UK lost for words?" she asked teasingly but with the guile of someone having just executed a trap in a chess move.

"Hotshot lawyer may have more words than he considers it wise to utter."

Oh she gave me a wonderful smile, her mouth joyously executing her next move. "Look, if I am to be your muse, you must be able to express yourself to me," said she as she leaned forward squeezing her hands between her knees, and tilting her head to one side as if to say, 'I'm waiting.'

"You want the details of what I found amazing about that encounter?" With her cigarette giving off an unusual aroma from her left hand, Elena gestured with her right hand as if to say 'come on, express yourself' with her facial expression entreating me. "Ok! What I found amazing about that encounter was this." I leaned to her to engage closer and she to me, our faces just a couple of feet apart as if a secret was to be shared. "To me it was a special moment. I felt privileged to have a glimpse and momentarily be part of someone else's private world. Not specifically for the nudity and my brief glimpse gave me only a general picture in that respect anyway, but for the event itself. Two people, both wanting solitude, come upon each other coincidentally and both surely having their senses heightened, she by being startled by a stranger of the opposite sex in her private world and he similarly by catching a glimpse of her. And yet she wasn't threatened in any way and there was no intrusion beyond the initial sighting. There was the simplest acknowledgement between us of understanding. To me, the chance encounter and the awareness it created, charging the senses, was a moment that added to the beauty of our surroundings. Yes it was the moment, the encounter itself that I found amazing and quite beautiful."

She looked into me intensely for a few moments and then with a wry smile said, "Hotshot lawyer uses the words of a skilled poet to get out of that one."

"Ok, I'll confess. God you looked amazing!"

We both laughed together. "Ok, you've passed that one," she said.

"Oh, it was a little test was it? Blackmail if I want you as a muse."

"I love your words and your thoughts and I want to be your muse and if it entails blackmail, so be it! Most men would have walked across that cove with their head permanently turned towards me. If he was Greek, he would have come over to me and chatted me up whilst hoping for a closer look – a true expression of his innate romantics. You did neither."

"I am not Greek and I am not most men," I told her.

"I know you are not most men," she said, again looking into my eyes thoughtfully.

"So – to go back to where we were. Not three but four different Elenas then and each one seemingly a different person and amazing in her own right but as I have said, I'm intrigued.

Do you consciously change your appearance for the task in hand?"

She smiled thoughtfully. "That's an interesting one. Yes, to some extent I do, particularly for my work. In my uniform I become that roll, the person I have to be in that world. Here in my home, the taverna, the village, the beach, I am variations on a theme." She laughed as if becoming aware of the significance herself and she saw me deep in thought. "What are you thinking, Matt?"

"Yes, I do find it intriguing. People operating in different worlds, alter egos, what we make ourselves or what we become. We're talking psycho-analysis basically which is a lengthy debate and probably for another day but it is another day that I would look forward to."

"I've never talked about that before but with you I would find it interesting." She picked up her coffee cup and holding it out towards me she said, "To another day."

"To another day," I said touching her cup with mine and I gestured to Marin for the bill.

"Are… are you in tonight Matt – in the taverna?" she asked, somewhat wistfully.

"Yes. Yes I am. Would you like to have a brandy together?"

"Yes I would," she replied with a smile. I have to meet someone at seven to give an English lesson for about an hour but I will come straight back. I'll see you then."

Chapter 9

Having my evening meal in the taverna, I looked up to see Elena behind the bar at the far end and she waved. She had obviously been looking but didn't want to disturb me. I put my arm up and pointed down to the empty seat at my table and she nodded with a big smile and came over to me.

"Hi Matt," said she.

"Have you eaten?" I asked as I stood up.

"I had some soup before I went but that is all."

"Will you have something with me?"

"I'd love to," she said enthusiastically. She turned round to attract someone's attention at the bar but there was no-one there at that moment. She backed up a couple of steps to me, comically leaned backwards, turning her face to mine and said, "I'll just tell them they're on their own now and to get some food here bloody quick," and then she made for the bar. She was delightful.

"So you are doing some teaching," I said once we were seated.

"I have a few clients for private lessons which I fit in with my work. It's good fun."

"Would you like another client?" She looked at me quizzically. "Teach me Greek. I have an online course arranged but I could use some practical assistance I'm sure."

"Seriously?" her face lit up. "I'd love to." And then she said, "Mm, my duties are increasing by the hour – muse, teacher…"

She was interrupted as several small dishes of food were brought to her. We ate together and with what remained of mine soon eaten, she insisted on me trying some of hers.

When we had finished, she asked, "Shall we have our coffee and brandy outside? Then I can have a cigarette."

We sat at a small table against the side of the taverna which was private and with a dimly lit lantern on the wall it was intimate in the balmy night air. As the village was virtually silent during the day, so it was at night but it was a different silence with the darkness cloaking everything about us. A large pot of coffee and the brandy was brought to us and Elena took out her cigarettes offering one to me. I shook my head but took her lighter and lit hers for her as a friendly gesture.

"I'm working tomorrow," she said, her voice sounding almost apologetic. "I'll be away for a few days. I drive to Thessaloniki and we're taking one of the smaller charter jets to Athens with some V.I.P's. then we have some meetings before flying back. Mine is an ambassadorial role. That's a good word isn't it," said she as she wet her finger and made a figure one in the air.

"Will you be in uniform?"

"Oh yes. All the time and talking of uniform, you saw me going off to the photo shoot, let me show you the airlines advertisement. She brought her phone to life and showed me a poster. "That's last year's," she said, "but the new one will be similar."

It was Elena in her uniform, seeming to be on top of a mountain, the breeze blowing the tails of her silk scarf and her hands outstretched, with the caption 'COME FLY WITH ME.'

"I like that! Is that the poster I will see on billboards?"

"Yes, everywhere and in the press, magazines and travel brochures. And this is the one you won't see," said she as she pulled up the next one. Before showing it to me she said, "The publicity boys know that I get fed up with being touched on the planes so as a joke they came up with this one." The picture of Elena on the mountain was the same but the caption was different. It read, 'MY NAME IS ELENA WITH ME YOU CAN FLY BUT TOUCH MY BOTTOM AND HOPE TO DIE.' I laughed. It was brilliant. "That is *not* in circulation but there is one on the wall of the publicity office and I have one in my room. I've also been told that at least one of the directors has a copy in his private collection," she said.

"Thanks for showing me that. Is it really an issue – being touched?"

"It's an occupational hazard," said she with a wonderful expression on her face. I obviously took too long to respond to that one and must have had a telling expression on *my* face. "Ok, what are you thinking now?"

"I'm not telling you."

"Look, you've got to enter into the spirit of this muse thing and express yourself," said she smiling all over her face.

"Being my muse doesn't give you full access to my mind," I told her. "A muse is not a confessor."

She burst out laughing, put her face to mine and said, "We'll see about that!" We laughed together. She was lovely. As the laughter subsided, she said in a softened tone, "Please tell me, Matt."

"That's a tricky one legally…"

"You weren't thinking of the legal position, Matt Rochester. You were thinking men's thoughts."

"And men's thoughts interest you."

"Yours do. You're not most men."

"Ok. Let's do that one again. Rewind!"

"In my work, being touched is an occupational hazard," she said, repeating herself with renewed emphasis.

"Mm, I can't help thinking it might have something to do with the way you fill that uniform."

She laughed and laughed. "Do you know Matt, from our conversations, I've formed the opinion that you should be writing. But you definitely need me as your muse!"

"And how fitting that my muse should be Greek. Muses originate in Greek mythology I recall."

"Yes. Goddesses of inspiration. They were the nine daughters of Zeus, king of the Gods."

"So I know who I'm talking to."

"Exactly."

"Ok, you've got the job," I confirmed and we shook hands playfully." But holding her hand over the table didn't transmit as playful. In that brief moment something passed between us. I couldn't readily define it but it felt warm and very special. Our interaction had changed. Our heads were closer, our voices softer and in the darkness of the night, it felt intimate.

She offered her cigarette for me to puff, which this time I took. It was indeed aromatic with clove being obvious but in a pleasant way and what other unspecified ingredients there were, added to that pleasantness. I felt an immediate uplift and a little heady but as I don't smoke very often I could put that down to the shock to the system which is normal. As I gave it back to her she looked into me with a trace of a smile then she turned her head away to stop it breaking out.

67

"Indonesia, you say."

"The crews bring them back for me." Again she was trying to stop a laugh breaking out. "They could help you to become a free spirit again, Matt."

"I don't doubt that."

"It must have been a huge decision for you – making a new start."

"Yes of course but it was formed over a long period of time – there was no sudden decision. But I tell you there was one thing that was a cathartic moment for me. I actually considered putting a roof rack on my car and bolting a surfboard to it to be permanently there."

"Street cred."

"No – Life cred. I was to put it there as a feel-good factor for me. It would be psychological but signifying to me that I had another life.

"Amazing psychology. Like my change of clothes and make-up."

"In a way but yours is real. Mine would have been psycho-babble. Frightening! The fact that I was even thinking about it told me it was time to do something about it. I literally looked in the mirror and said 'get real.' So here I am and it's not predominantly to surf. It's to regain the free spirit that I once was."

"Have you met Stefanos? He surfs."

"Yes I have. His bike brought us together. He's going to take me with him when the winds are right. I was surprised to learn that that there is surfing in Greece."

"Oh great! You can also talk your eastern philosophies with him too. He has lived with the monks in the Far East."

"Really?"

"Yes. He's a lovely guy. You and he will be great together"

"He's seems for real."

"So are you Matt. He will probably show you his goats and his cats."

"Cats?"

"Yes, he has a small herd of goats and he loves his cats and they love him. You must know that Greece in general is alive with wild cats. Well he's adopted a few – actually they've adopted each other. They eat with him, sleep with him – they'd go surfing with him if they could." We laughed together.

"Have you played other sports Matt?"

"No, not really. Some tennis maybe."

"Not rugby?"

"Err, yes and no."

"You didn't like it."

"I played at school because I had to, or I was expected to do so. Did I enjoy it? – No! Was I good at it? – No! One of my fellow students summed it up brilliantly when he uttered the words, 'Eleven silly buggers chasing a bag of wind!' He got detention for that." Elena laughed. "Again, it alienated my innate sense of justice and fair play for the individual. If somebody gets the ball, take a running dive at them to bring them down and get it off them and if you're not immediately successful, let everyone else pile on top of him. I was told that it's endemic in our culture – passed down from the nobility. A tradition. I reckon it therefore stemmed from medieval warfare. In medieval times men were killing men in battle. When there was no war they were killing animals for sport. Now they are not allowed to do that, they play rugby!"

"*You* could have got detention for that?"

"I was careful what I said and to whom!"

"Just like all hotshot lawyers," said a highly amused Elena.

"How about you? I know you play games because you play games with me."

"You've noticed! I play chess but with you it's verbal chess." Between us we were almost in constant laughter. "I practise yoga. I'm into it and have been for many years. It's a connection – mind and body and all that there is about us. It's very important for me."

"I get that totally."

"Also, I do like to swim," she said. "I love to swim in the sea, as you do." She looked into me just a foot or so away and said, "Would you like to see my secret island?"

"You have a secret island?"

"Yes. Nobody else knows about it but I'd love to share it with you. It's north of here, about forty kilometres, in a very remote almost inaccessible region. There are no roads for the last part, just tracks, if that. The island is a rocky outcrop about the size of a football pitch and it has some vegetation on it and even a small sandy beach on its far side. – a world of its own. It's about five hundred metres off shore – a good swim."

"Wow! That sounds amazing. I'd love to experience it with you. Thank you."

I know you like wild swimming. It's not wild like the south west coast of England, the sea is warm and usually quite calm but it's a little adventure."

"It sounds magical."

"I'm away for four or five days. We could go when I come back."

"I will look forward to it – immensely!"

She put her hand on my arm as she said, "I must get some rest Matt. I have a long day tomorrow – the drive to Thessaloniki and then the preparation.

"Wouldn't you normally drive up the day before?"

"Yes, but that would have been today Matt and I didn't want to," said she looking into me. "Can we exchange telephone numbers and then we can keep in touch?"

"I was going to ask you but I thought maybe your own world is private."

"No," she said, holding out her hand for my phone. "What use is a muse if she's incommunicado?" We exchanged numbers then she stood up and looked into my face. She squeezed my arm and said softly, "Thanks for today Matt and thanks for the conversation. I've enjoyed it immensely."

"Me too, Elena. Thank you so much for your company and showing me around."

"I'll be in touch," she whispered and turned to walk away.

"Elena," I called. She stopped, turned and looked to me. "Take care," I told her with sincerity.

She came back up to me and said, "You too, Matt," and then she put her head to mine, gently touched my cheek with her lips and whispered, "See you soon."

Chapter 10

I saw Jennifer most days and we would invariably have a little chat. "Would you like to see my villa? – have a look round," she asked on the last such occasion.

"Yes, I'd like that very much," I replied.

"I'm back to the UK tomorrow for a few days – say my hellos, a couple of meetings and tie up a few loose ends. It also serves to reinforce my conviction that this is where I prefer to be," she said.

"You know that in advance?"

"Absolutely. No question," added she with a smile. "We could arrange something when I come back."

"I'll look forward to it."

Stefanos telephoned me to say that the winds were forecast to be favourable for surfing over the next few days, and not by coincidence I thought, he suggested the day after Jennifer was leaving for the UK.

I had a text from Alex:

Hello Matt. How have you settled in? Is the area and taverna to your liking?

Is it a place that might suit you long term? Be good to hear from you! Alex

To me, it was significant that he didn't mention Jennifer and I was glad that he didn't. I didn't want to get involved in that. In the absence of hearing from me, I would expect him to send such a text but I couldn't help feeling that the timing was to do with Jennifer's forthcoming return to the UK when I was pretty sure they would meet up. I would give myself a bit of time to consider my response before replying.

I also had a text from Elena, which was lovely:

Hi Matt. Busy days, meetings and more meetings (yes mostly in uniform!!!) but going well. Will be another day or two before I fly back – will text you when. Loved our conversations and looking forward to our swim to the secret island if you're still on! Have you got that title yet? Elena.

Yes it was lovely – chatty and meaningful and I would reply spontaneously without the need for consideration.

Hi Elena. Thanks for your message. Glad you're ok. Yes I loved our conversations too and of course I'm on for the island and looking forward to it very much. I'm surfing with Stefanos day after tomorrow. No title yet but writing. (You should need a licence to wear that uniform!!!) Take care. Matt.

Stefanos was to pick me up in the taverna car park and as he drove in I was amazed at what I saw. He had an old Citroen 2CV van or the deux cheveaux as they were known in France. And it *was* old – they stopped making them about thirty years ago from my memory and this looked like one of the earlier models. Designed for simplicity and economy, it was the quintessential French workhorse – so beloved by farmers and small traders. The van section was built of corrugated steel and gave a very utilitarian boxy appearance – often referred to as the tin snail. Regarded as a mass produced classic, in later years it gained cult status. To the motoring snobs it was the epitome of naffness but to the more perceptive, its minimalist charm translated to French chic – in this case, shabby chic. It was unpretentious and with his surf boards on the roof rack, for Stefanos it was the perfect fit.

"Hi Stefanos – love your wheels!"

"Hi Matt," was his response, with his hand held out for a hit. "Yeah, I love it too! I've spent time with some monks in the Far East and that sorted what I need in this world and shiny cars aren't part of it. It works! Plenty of room in the back for gear or tools and the roof rack for the surf boards and long pieces of timber."

With a squeak and the sound of hollow metal, he opened the rear doors and put my bag in with his kite surfing gear that he had brought as an option if the waves were not right for surfing.

Getting underway, the engine sounded like that of a lawn mower but seeing Stefanos nonchalantly wrapped around the steering wheel, much the same as he is over a table when eating a meal – cool came to mind!

"We're going south, about an hour down the coast. There's a small headland there and with the right wind, the currents and the sea bed usually make for good waves with a long run. If it's not

72

right, we'll kite surf," said he with a nod towards the back of the van.

"Great," I responded as we trundled along to an engine sound that would suggest a speed of at least twice that of what we were actually doing but the ride was supreme. The seats were comfortable and the soft suspension giving a floaty ride. "So… monks. You've lived with them. A monastery?"

He turned to me momentarily and nodded.

"Yeah man. I…" he hesitated to find words. "I had a good education in Greece but I dropped out. I couldn't settle. I spent some time in Thailand but things didn't immediately work out for me. The beauty and the peace that I wanted didn't happen. The Shaolin community there helped me and eventually I went to one of their temples." He looked at me again briefly with a grimace before adding, "I needed help and they took me in. I lived, isolated with them for two years and I found the peace and beauty and the understanding of life that I went out to the Far East for in the first place. Peace and beauty, man! Solitude, simple healthy diet, no possessions, the awareness of reality." He turned to me briefly again and I saw a quality in him that was awesome – serenity, but his presence was enormous. I could feel his presence but it didn't project – there was no ego. He had his own understanding, his own world and it was completely natural. He wasn't acting or trying to be anything. He wasn't convincing himself or following a creed. He simply was! And with my basic understanding of the eastern philosophies, I felt privileged to be with him – to interact with him and be part of his world.

"Was it very isolated?"

"Believe it! Just a small mountain community nearby. Nothing else anywhere near. We grew our own vegetables and herbs, practised natural healing and meditation."

"Two years is a long time."

"It took six months to get the modern world out of me. The crap," he added as he again turned his face to mine.

"Did you train as a monk?"

"No. That wasn't my intention and besides that's ten years just to get initiated. But I trained in their practices and lived their lifestyle. It's a philosophy, man. To seek reality."

73

"I understand Stefanos. I've always had a leaning that way. I've read up on Eastern philosophies and the Buddhist teachings. I don't have your experience and depth of understanding but I get it."

"I know you do man. I'm Stefan to my friends," he said and he put his hand up for an acknowledgement. "You're a lawyer I'm told. Here for a new life."

"That puts it well and I'm grateful for your friendship."

"Me too man. How do you like the taverna?"

"I love it – location, ambience, food and Maya, Elena and the staff are great. If I settle I may well look for a villa."

"You've met Jennifer. She bought a villa. I'm helping with the renovation – the woodwork. A lot to be done."

"Yes, so I hear. She's offered to show it to me when she comes back. I hear you're good with wood."

"I love it. I did a lot in the Far East. And it pays for some extras – like the Harley, which is my one material possession of the modern world. This is a necessity," said he, gesturing about the van "and it's so old, it's not really part of the modern world," he added with a laugh.

"The chic style that it represents is of the modern world. But I would suggest you bought it as a practical simplistic unpretentious workhorse, so it fits with your ethos."

"And it was cheap man. It was pulled out of a ditch."

"Seriously?"

"Seriously. I got it from the same garage that made the Harley a goer after its accident. The van's had some work done on it but to restore it to the standard of a valuable classic would take money I haven't got – not that I'd be interested in that. I love it the way it is – the dents, and the aged patina of dull, weathered paintwork and rust. My little farm and my goats pay for a simple existence."

"How did you come by your place?"

"At the monastery one day, I got a letter telling me an uncle had died back in Greece and had left it to me and a little money – enough to keep it running as a going concern. It's very basic – more like a humble shepherds dwelling with some land but I've got it how I like it and I don't want for more. I grow a lot of my stuff – I get by! It gave me the opportunity to come back to

Greece with a new start and a simple lifestyle that I wanted. It feels right!"

"Good for you Stefan. I'm pleased for you."

"I'll show you sometime. It's my monastic way of life. I'm careful about visitors – I don't want negative vibes but you're different. You're welcome matt."

"I'd like that – when it suits."

Although we were going at a leisurely pace, time soon passed and he turned off the road to what was more of a track and eventually the intense blue of the sea became visible in the distance. As we became more remote, the going got rougher but the soft suspension gave a strange but very comfortable ride. Even as we neared the beach, the van simply glided over the uneven ground and what seemed like shale.

We got out and Stefanos stood gazing out to sea, appraising the conditions. "Looks good to me," he said as we watched the wave formations out to the headland. "We need to paddle some way out to pick up the waves at source. Catch the right one out there and you get a long ride man. The seabed flattens out so once they start to break, they hold for some time."

The waves were some way out but looked sizeable and were breaking one after the other. "I'd say those waves are at least two metres," I suggested.

"Yeah, I guess," said he and we changed into our board shorts, and unstrapped the boards from the roof. "Give me a few minutes," he said and he made his way to the sea. He put down his board and his bag on the rocks and walked to the water's edge. He took up a stance and I knew he was going to do some kind of workout.

But this was no Kung Fu workout as I have seen them. This was not the preparation of a warrior but more of a tuning to the elements. He was becoming as one with all that was around him – harmonising. And what I saw was amazing. I've seen similar routines before but not of that perfection. He remained on one spot in perfect balance while his arms and body movements were very expressive as he both expelled and drew in forces. But what was most amazing to me was that all his movements were continuous from one to the other. Except for the occasional pause with perfect balance, there was no break. You could not discern the beginning or end of each movement. It was more ethereal than physical as if unknown energy was controlling his movements rather than his body, with his stillness and balance seemingly unreal. One could practice such movement for a very long time without achieving this result, such perfection can only come from within. He was but just two or three minutes before turning to me to signify he was ready. His face was absolute peace and his presence awesome.

We waded out together until we were waist deep then mounted our boards lying face down and paddled with our arms over the broken waves to the heavy swell beyond and conferred as we assessed the potential optimum point to try for the incoming rollers. It was so different to what I had grown used to off the north Cornish coast – the sea temperature far higher with no wet suits necessary, the waves although quite sizeable seemed to lack the ferocity of wilder seas and the colours were so vibrant.

Having caught consecutive waves we both arrived back near the beach more or less together after a long ride. "Hey man," said Stefan, holding out his hand for a hit, "you're good!"

"You too, Stefan," I acknowledged truthfully. He really looked the part – his poise, his balance, his whole stature and confidence. We eagerly headed out for more and we continued to surf for some three hours with just a short break.

"Are you hungry?" he asked as we arrived at the shore once more together. We hadn't brought food, just bottled water. Stefan said there was a little taverna up the coast to which we could easily divert on the way back.

"Yes. Yes I am. You?" He nodded with a huge smile. "Your taverna sounds good. Can I buy you some lunch?"

"Sounds great, man." I had offered to pay for the petrol but he wouldn't hear of it. "It cost me no more than if I come on my own," was his response. Sitting back in the slightly musty atmosphere of his old van – an atmosphere that no amount of cleaning would eradicate for it was surely endemic, I had the warm feeling of being cocooned. Being out of the elements, it felt a safe haven after taking on raw nature, the cacophony of the wind and breaking waves, the challenge, the thrills and the sheer exhilaration that we had experienced. All was now calm, still and quiet.

Stefan brought the 'lawn mower engine' to life and we set off over some rough ground, tracks then minor roads to the little beachside taverna that he knew. It was an unassuming place, quite small with a few tables inside but most out, which were of bare wood, some with plastic table cloths. With a few people seated, it brought us back to civilisation somewhat as Stefan had a hearty conversation with the owner in their native tongue – they clearly knew each other well. He introduced me and we touched fists – his English was very limited.

"The food is ok here and the chips are good." Said Stefan.

"You like chips?"

"I love chips man! But they have to be right."

"Chips seem to play a large part in Greek cuisine," I said.

"Yeah, that's right. Chips everywhere but they vary."

"Do you cook them yourself at home?"

"No. I don't really fry much but I have them where I know they are good – like Maya's. They're very good."

We had vegetable pizza with the chips – we'd worked up an appetite. Stefan doesn't drink much alcohol he tells me so we both had lime infused carbonated mineral water.

"Tell me Stefan, your little ritual. Feng shui?

"Qigong," he confirmed. "Similar – it's practised alongside Kung Fu in the monasteries."

"Do you practice actual Kung Fu as it is known?"

He looked at me intently. "Yes, big time. I studied for years even before the monastery. It's a big part of my life – my discipline."

"So you say you didn't study to become a monk but you follow Buddhist principles?"

"Right!" It's my life man."

The food *was* good and it looked amazing with the chips, slithers of potato lightly golden with a good texture. Stefan adopted his usual posture – wrapped around his meal, his left arm on the table steadying his plate whilst he ate solely with the fork in his right hand picking up the food from the back of the plate having cut the pizza before he started. I could imagine him eating in the monastery in the same posture with his food in a bowl and using just his right hand with chopsticks.

"Tell me. Stefan. I see your detachment from the modern world. Is it something you constantly have to work at or is it something that you have become. That you are almost in another dimension?"

He smiled at me. A beautiful smile, his face absolute serenity. "You ask me questions like nobody has before," he said. "You have a great awareness Matt." He took a moment to consider his reply, to choose his words. "I think so far as other dimensions are concerned, it's not cut and dried. To me I'm on a spectrum." He gestured with his arms, drawing his hands apart as if stretching the space between them to qualify his meaning of a spectrum. Aware of other dimensions, I am not fully in any of them, including our own. I drift along that spectrum but with great awareness. We are all multi-dimensional beings operating on a physical plane but developing and exercising greater awareness with time."

"I understand. Thanks!"

"I know you do, man. Nobody else does – maybe Jennifer. It's the gift of being in the monastery with the monks."

"Does Jennifer share your beliefs?"

"Yeah, pretty much, I'd say. She's got to know me well. We have long chats."

"Buddhists believe that our attachment to people and things is the reason for our suffering," I put to him, "and to obtain enlightenment we should adopt non-attachment. How do you see that?"

"Buddhists see the origin of unhappiness in attachments and that we should let go of material possessions, emotions, desires. This enables an inner peace – contentment from within and greater awareness."

"And relationships with people?"

"There are no rules man – just principles and we apply those according to our awareness. A relationship with someone can be an attachment with commitment, the controlling and the jealousies. Or it can be a sharing of each moment with understanding in an ever changing world." He turned to me and smiled. But it wasn't a contrived smile. The smile I saw was a projection of peace and serenity from within. His presence was

78

like no other I have known. He was so real, so natural, so unaffected. What he gave off was there to be understood.

I thought of his relationship with Jennifer. It didn't need greater definition other than a sharing of meaningful moments together which may be of the moment or ongoing. By his creed it could be non-attachment. We continued to chat on the drive back and he was keen to understand my potential transition from London lawyer to writer in remote Greece. It was meaningful and with great depth. I had a friend such that I hadn't had for a long time and it was good.

"Thanks Stefan," I told him as he dropped me off at the taverna. "Thanks for a great day! The use of your board, the surfing and your company."

"Hey, thank *you* man and thanks for the lunch," he said, responding with a meaningful hug. "We'll do it again and kite surfing when it's right."

I had another message from Elena and it gave me a warm glow:

Hi Matt. Coming home tomorrow so secret island the next day if that's ok. Elena.

I replied:

Hi Elena. Yes great! Looking forward to seeing you. Matt

Over my evening meal in the taverna I gave great thought to Alex's text. The timing of it just before Jennifer's visit to the UK made it more informative by what he didn't say. He was in fact asking about Jennifer without mentioning her, which he obviously didn't feel it wise to spell out. I really didn't want to get involved in that scenario – there was no obligation to do so, not even an understanding. I saw my only possible obligation was to thank him for telling me about the area and the taverna.

I replied: *Hello Alex. Good to hear from you. Early days but first impressions all good. Beautiful area and the taverna is a gem! Still acclimatising but enjoying the climate, the swimming and starting to write. Am grateful for the recommendation. We must meet up when I visit the UK. Matt.*

I was aware too that my text was conspicuous without the mention of Jennifer and would probably fall short of his expectations but as I saw it I was damned if I did and damned if I didn't. Jennifer was a factor in the equation for Alex even if she wasn't for me. As I realised at the outset there was always a potential 'can of worms' there and whatever I said or didn't say wasn't going to make it go away.

Stefanos had advised of favourable winds and they enabled us to surf. He would be unaware of a less favourable wind, an ill wind the possible stirrings of which I was becoming uncomfortably aware – the wisps silently permeating my senses like the scent of a smoking candle in the breeze. I sensed the possibility of a storm brewing from beyond the horizon and this tranquil haven on the Adriatic Sea was in its path.

Chapter 11

As I was enjoying my breakfast, I got a text from Elena:
Arrived Thessaloniki. About to drive home. Brandy tonight?
I felt a warm glow. I'd been looking forward to seeing her again and confirmation that she was back and the thought of her company thrilled me. I replied immediately:
Absolutely! But I will be eating in the taverna as usual if you're free!
I had hardly returned my phone to my pocket when the reply came:
I didn't like to presume. See you soon!
Although anticipated, her appearance in the taverna was a jolt to my senses and as we made eye contact the smile on her face was lovely – her joy was to behold as she came up to me from behind the bar.

"Hi Matt," she said, as she held my arms and put her cheek to mine momentarily. And it was just a moment but in that second or two I smelled her subtle perfume and her hair. But more than that, I sensed something that I couldn't immediately define. It was a combination of her scent with something of her presence. I thought about it. It was the aura of a person well-travelled and fresh from the business world. The text books don't have it but I know that if she had been at home all day, her same greeting would have presented very differently to the senses. It was more than the effect of her return after being away for a few days. It was more like the sum of what she had experienced having affected her aura. Was it just aromas, the infusion of a corporate world still lingering. I thought it more. I thought of it as other subtle influences such as vibes or intuition – of a science not yet known to man. And although she is back in her home environment, her aura needs time to assimilate.

"Are you ok?" I asked. "Have you enjoyed your mission?"

"Yes I have," she replied, adding "but it's good to be back," looking at me with her head slightly canted.

"It's lovely to see you, Elena. Thanks for keeping in touch."

We found a table and when we sat down I put to her my thoughts about her aura and she knew exactly what I meant. She told me that at the airline, with close proximity it was often possible to tell whether a person was coming on duty or finishing a shift and she too had thought it more than aroma.

"It probably has something to do with personas. Of being different people at different times," I put to her.

"So what person am I at this moment?" asked she with a curious look.

"You are in transition," I told her.

"Some and some," she proffered.

"A mixed bag!" I qualified.

Did she laugh! She found that highly amusing. And then her face straightened and looking directly into me she said, "Be very careful Matt Rochester," and then she burst out laughing again.

"So your trip was busy but enjoyable?"

"Y-e-s," she said, drawing out the word as if to imply it needed some qualification. "We took the 'Gulfstream' down to Athens, as you know. Potential clients discussing private charter on a regular basis."

"VIPs?"

"Very much so! I can't disclose," said she apologetically.

"How many does it seat?"

"Fourteen. They can experience the aircraft, the hospitality and the cuisine, which is quite special – much like that of a private yacht. Then we had meetings in Athens and when I wasn't directly involved I did some work on the training manuals. Yes, it's interesting – another world and it went well," said she with the implication of a job well done. "And talking of cuisine, what will you eat tonight? You're into vegetables aren't you?" She then put her finger up and said, "Let me arrange a few dishes for us."

"Yes, I'd like that," I told her and she went into the kitchen to arrange things.

"So how was your surfing with Stefanos," she asked as she re-seated herself opposite me at our table.

"Really good. Very different to North Cornwall but so enjoyable. No wet suit, warm water, balmy winds and stunningly clear air. It's been a long time and I didn't expect it in Greece and Stefan is great company. I really like the Guy. He's so real."

"And he likes you – I knew he would."

"Why do you say that?"

"Well he asked you surfing for one thing. He's very much a loner – he doesn't have friends that I know of. And you refer to him as Stefan obviously at his suggestion. The only other person that I know who calls him Stefan is Jennifer. I knew you two would become friends and I'm so pleased for both of you."

"He wants to show me his home."

"Wow. That will be interesting."

"Have you seen it?"

"No. And he hasn't suggested I call him Stefan." Then she gave me a tight smile and added, "Maybe I should learn surfing and talk philosophy." Then she laughed and said, "He really is a lovely guy – we get on well. Did you take lunch with you? I think that where he surfs is very remote."

"Yes it is but he knew of a little taverna on the way back with a slight deviation."

"Good?"

"Yes. Not like this but ok. He likes his chips as many Greek people do. They are very much part of the cuisine here aren't they."

Just as I completed that sentence the food was brought to us and several bowls set out on our table, including a bowl of chips. And they looked good, typically long wedge shaped and a light golden colour suggesting a slight crispiness but a soft texture within.

"You like chips!"

"I love chips and especially here in Greece. Some food writers have gone as far as to say that Greek chips are the best in the world. Why are they different?"

We helped ourselves to some of the dishes as Elena explained. "It comes down to several things. Firstly the potatoes. There are one or two types here that make particularly good chips but most importantly it is the preparation and the cooking. The chips are usually soaked in water before cooking. That is important to reduce the starch – they fry much better. Then we shallow fry them in olive oil. We have plenty of olive oil here in Greece. We use extra virgin because it doesn't break down under normal cooking temperatures and it puts more flavour in the chips."

She smiled at me as if to say – there is your answer.

"In England, chips have had the reputation of being fatty things that you eat out of newspaper with battered fish and are bad for your health, but I think they have improved somewhat nowadays. We have the so called gourmet chip but they're not as nice as these."

"Here they are simply potatoes and olive oil and if not cooked at too high a temperature form an acceptable part of the everyday diet."

I took a chip from the bowl and held it out to her before putting it in my mouth. "Cheers," I said. "Mm, I've enjoyed them here several times but these seem extra special – probably because of you describing the process. I can taste the subtle olive oil."

Elena smiled and nodded. "It is important to change the oil regularly!"

"This is all lovely – the vegetables, the filo pastry. Thank you."

"Thank you for the wine Matt." I'd ordered a bottle that I knew was a favourite of hers. to celebrate her return.

My phone came to life – an incoming message.

"Do you want to take it," asked Elena, seeing that I hadn't responded to it.

"No. I have more important matters here at the moment," I told her. "I'm not on twenty four hour call."

She gave me an endearing smile and looked into me in a very expressive way, appreciative that our meal together and our conversation was more important to me than an incoming message. And that was true but what she didn't know was that on hearing my phone, I had an inner feeling that the sender was Alex and I certainly wasn't going to interrupt my evening to read that. I was doing some work for a client but they would communicate by email. A text and in the evening would almost certainly be a response from Alex, particularly knowing he would have probably seen Jennifer now. I would wait till I was in my room.

"So tomorrow," said Elena with enthusiasm. "I can't wait to go swimming with you and show you the island and the journey up there is a little adventure. I suggest we take my car – I've got a four-by-four and some of the route is off the beaten track,"

"Yes, whatever you think. Is that your jeep that I've seen parked outside?"

"Yes quirky isn't it but it's a refined small jeep and I love it."

"Yes I understand but it's not as quirky as Stefan's van."

"Oh I know. Wonderful isn't it. And isn't it just him?"

"Absolutely."

"My film crew saw it outside with the surfboards on top last year and were blown away. They pictured it on a beach at sunset and when I described Stefanos to them, they wanted him in it as well. I mentioned it to him but he didn't want to know" Then she mimicked him, quite demonstrably saying "No way man!" We laughed together. I could well appreciate Stefan's reaction.

"So what time do we get underway?"

"Coffee and breakfast eight o'clock and then we go," said she with an enthusiasm that suggested disappointment that we were having to wait until morning before we were setting off.

"What can I bring to the party?"

"Nothing. Just yourself," she said affectionately. "Don't forget your board shorts," she added softly and with an intonation suggestive that without them there would be a crisis, "and your towel. I'll bring the lunch for us – there's nowhere to eat within miles and that way we are independent."

"Please charge that to my room plus the food this evening."

"No way. It's my treat."

"I insist!" I told her. "Particularly if we're using your car." She touched my hand on the table and smiled.

We went outside and sat at a small table at the side of the taverna for the brandy. The darkness, inky black but for the dim lantern on the wall above us and a sky full of stars suggesting a portal to infinity, and our space together felt other-worldly in the cool air. She offered me a cigarette. I shook my head but picked up her lighter and lit hers – one of her black variety as usual.

"Indonesia you say."

"Something like that," she smiled.

She offered me the odd puff as we sipped our brandy. Her presence fused with the atmosphere and was mesmerising. I

85

became aware of a rarefied moment and my concentration drifted.

"What?" she asked.

I came back to the moment, looked into her, took her cigarette momentarily for a puff and returning it to her I told her, "There are occasionally very meaningful moments in this world and this is one of them. I love being with you and I'm really looking forward to tomorrow."

"Me too Matt," she said looking into me. "I thought of you a lot while I was away."

"Thanks again for keeping in touch. I… that was nice."

"I wanted to," she said and then lightening the mood she continued, "we've got a whole day tomorrow…"

In my room I checked my phone. It was indeed Alex:

Hello Matt. So glad you are settling in, I was confident it would be to your liking. You didn't mention Jennifer. I was with her today and I have to say she is a different person. Absolutely radiant. Her skin, smiling eyes with enlarged pupils and a demeanour that has been lost to her for years. Obviously you have got together and I'm pleased for you both. Credit me for my placement skills! Alex

I smiled to myself. Not by way of feeling pleasure but by recognition of the way wheels turn in this world, the ironies and the inevitabilities but behind my smile was an anxiety. The smoke from my candle in the breeze was dancing playfully like a genie out of a lamp given freedom to express itself and with a message of foreboding – it was not difficult to sense its aroma turning acrid. I would give careful consideration to my reply in the morning but fully aware that my options were limited – confirm

Chapter 12

I replied to Alex's message in the only way possible for me – telling the truth. I wasn't going to dig myself in deeper by appeasing him and I certainly wasn't going to tell tales.

Alex, I'm pleased to hear that you find Jennifer radiant and expressing a satisfaction with life. I cannot however take credit for it. Yes I have met her and we've had the occasional brief conversation but nothing beyond that and certainly not any form of relationship. I can only think that what you have seen is the result a lifestyle that suits her here and in particular the love of the renovation of her villa, about which she is passionate. Matt

Elena's jeep was lovely. Not of the military type but a definite jeep appearance in a refined way and apart from its practicality, it gave character to a lady of Elena's lifestyle. It was in burnt orange, chic, and was a broad fit across the different Elenas I knew.

With our bags stowed we set off with Elena looking very confident and competent behind the wheel. She had shown me on the map where we were headed, the secret island showing just as a dot off a headland. It was to be about an hour's drive north up the coast with the last part of it being off the beaten track as she had said. She was just as chatty while driving, pointing out things of interest and always with her sense of humour not far away.

"Did you have long philosophical conversations with Stefanos," she asked.

"Yes I certainly did."

"Good?"

"Yes. He's got it together and genuinely lives his life in peace and harmony. He wants for nothing. That's something he has got from his time in the monasteries with the monks."

"Yes, that is what he went to the Far East to find. He had a good education here in Greece but couldn't settle – I think he was desperate to get out of the system. A common problem of thinking too deeply." She looked at me with an expression as if to say ring any bells?

"Yes it sounds as though he dropped out early whereas I joined the system to drop out at a later date."

She smiled, put her hand on my thigh and squeezed it. "So do you share all of his beliefs – non-attachment for instance?"

"So you know of his beliefs?"

"Only in general from the brief chats we've had."

"Mm. Non-attachment is not easily explained or understood. Yes, the monks believe that the source of all our woes is because of our attachments – things, possessions, relationships. They say that we should observe as a third party, remaining mobile as we experience life's journey."

"So do you share that belief Matt?"

"I understand the philosophy but the extent to which any of us practice it either by design or by default is difficult to define."

"You are ducking the question Matt Rochester."

"No. No I'm not. I fully understand the principal and its possible implications but I am not a monk and neither is Stefan. We each determine the degrees of our attachments as we progress on life's journey according to our understanding and our awareness at the time."

"So would you not have a relationship, for instance?"

"Some monks marry. It's not an absolute. There are relationships and relationships. Their beliefs are woven into their relationships. They all have the beliefs but they adapt to what is right for them at the time."

"You still haven't answered my question."

"Yes, yes I would have a relationship – perhaps even need one!"

"But with detachment?"

"Hey! Stop trying to nail me to the wall Elena Costopolou." She laughed and again put her hand on my thigh and squeezed it. "Look, I don't have any fixed viewpoints, ok? I'm not a monk and not even close." She laughed again, delighting in teasing me to extract my thoughts. I put my hand on her thigh and was about to say more but the words wouldn't come. My mind was telling me that whatever I said would translate to non-attachment. She had dug me into a pit. "Look," I told her, "just drive the bloody car, ok?"

She laughed and laughed, the car deviating from a straight line before she pulled in and turned to look at me. "Look, I'm teasing you, ok?"

"Ok! Fun is it?"

"Yes," she replied, still laughing. And as we got underway she added, "I'll stick to driving the bloody car." She turned her head to look at me momentarily, snorting with tight lips as she tried to restrain her laugh, before turning again to the road ahead.

The roads declined from main to minor ones and then eventually a track through a wooded area before coming to an unmade but hard terrain. If there was a track it was barely discernible being the remnants of a means long gone. The satnav was useless here with Elena basically following a compass point until after several miles the coastline came into view giving a reference for her steering.

"How did you find this in the first place," I asked.

"My adventurous spirit. I love looking at maps and finding places to explore – the more remote, the better. I found the headland and then saw the little island. The headland seemed remote enough but the island looked off the map – undiscovered."

We drove down a slope which took us almost to the beach where she parked and the little island was clearly in view. We got out and surveyed the scene. All around the promontory the Aegean dazzled with an intense blue in the sunlight, the land around us was rocky and sandy with sparse vegetation. The island appeared simply as a large rock protruding from the sea with some vegetation on it and the senses were teased with heat haze here and there.

"Wow," I said. "Some place. Beyond civilisation, desolate but incredibly beautiful. It must have taken some courage for you to consider swimming out there on your own the first time – it's some way off."

"Yes, I was uncertain but I went for a swim, found myself further and further out until I thought just go for it. Are you still up for it?"

"Absolutely!"

"I thought you would be. Come," she said and we walked to the back of the jeep where she opened her bag and took out her things. She took off her denim shorts and her white blouse to reveal her bikini underneath. It was a modest bikini, designed for swimming rather than skimpy sunbathing but it was quality, fitted her well and was flattering with her figure. With her black hair flowing and dark skin, she looked superb. I walked to the other side of the jeep to put on my board shorts and when I rejoined her she showed me her swim bags. "Have you used these before," she asked?

"No, I don't think I have."

"They're completely waterproof and have buoyancy so we can take our towels, the lunch, phones and personal things with us. I've got two, so one each. Also. They're bright orange which should identify us if a boat comes along while we're halfway across but I've never seen one around here or another living soul."

"Brilliant," I told her and we strapped them round our waists to tow them on their long lead and set off. The water was warm, needing no acclimatisation and we were soon swimming side by side with a mixture of breaststroke and front crawl. The island did seem a long way off at sea level but we persevered having the occasional chat as we progressed. I put my head under and reckoned the depth to be some twenty feet or more with a variety of marine life in attendance. As we got further out the water seemed to have more swell but there was little wind. "Have you been aware of any currents here," I asked her.

"No," she replied. "I think it might depend on the conditions but whenever I've been and certainly today, you can aim for a spot and swim straight."

We were heading to round the island on its right side because the little beach where we could land was on the far side she told me. As we started to round the island we did notice a slight pull in the water so we put our heads down and did front crawl until we were on the far side. She was a good swimmer, good style and effective and with a confidence that she would have needed to attempt such a swim in the first place. It took us a good half an hour in all before we were walking up the small beach, the mainland now behind the island out of sight.

"I feel like Robinson Crusoe coming ashore on the unknown," I said.

"Isn't it amazing," she replied, beaming all over her face. "I've done it a few times now and I always get that same feeling I got the first time."

We set out our towels and sat next to each other, utterly alone and with a feeling of total isolation, with most probably no other beings within miles and miles from where we parked the car on the headland and from there we have swum for half an hour to a tiny island out to sea – a world of its own. She was looking at me. "You look good in your board shorts," she said. "They're classy. They suit you – dark navy and a super fit."

"Ah – thanks! You look really good in your bikini. That's classy too and fits you well."

"Thanks Matt. You're a discerning person – I value your opinion. This is my swimming bikini. I have others, for sunbathing or less purposeful swimming."

"And no bikini for some swimming."

She laughed. You don't know whether I swam on that occasion."

"Yes I do."

"You didn't see me swimming," said she with smug satisfaction.

"I didn't need to. As I crossed the cove I saw wet footprints in the sand from the sea to where you were."

"I could have taken my bikini off after my swim to sunbathe."

"There was no bikini to be seen and you wouldn't have put it in your bag while wet."

She smiled broadly but an artful smile. "Surprising what you can take in in a split second – isn't it!"

"Absolutely!"

"I'm going to rough you up Matt Rochester!" said she with menace.

"I'd think very carefully about that before you try."

"Mm. Ok, I'll forgive you on this occasion," she said holding out her hand which I took and we shook hands with great laughter.

She shuffled up closer so that our sides were almost touching and looking into me she said, "Matt, can I ask you something – something personal?"

"Try me."

"Are you in a relationship?"

"No. No I'm not," I answered sincerely.

"Have you been in one recently?"

"No."

"So you haven't come to Greece because of a broken relationship?"

"No – not at all."

She looked pleased. Pleased to have an answer to something that had obviously been on her mind. But she seemed hesitant, as though she wanted to ask more but couldn't find the words. I sensed she wanted to know more about me so in softened tones I talked to her. I told her of my long term relationship from university times and how it weakened as we matured and became different people. I told her in detail much as I had told Alex before I left England. How we grew apart and went our separate ways without a sudden break – without trauma or animosity. "That was some years ago now. I've missed having a relationship and as a man I've missed the physical side of things. Yes there are always women but I can't have a relationship unless it's the right person and I'm not into casual sex. And in its absence my mind has become ever more creative which has not been easy at times. In my work I have come across psychologists and psychiatrists who advocate acting out fantasies as a release – to prevent bottlenecks. But for me, any release would be in a relationship not as a means to an end."

Elena looked concerned and very thoughtful. "Matt, thank you for talking to me," she said.

"How about you? May I ask you the same question?" Looking as you do and with your personality and in your working environment you must have opportunities."

"Oh there are always men but I don't want that. I don't sleep around – I never have. I want more. I had an affair with a much older man – a married man. I was twenty two, he was in his early forties. He was an ex-pilot and an executive at the airline. At the outset it was quite passionate and he was going to leave his wife. It went on for over three years and for the last of those it was very much on and off. It went on for too long. He couldn't leave his wife and I wasn't sure that I wanted him to. He had children and I didn't want to be party to that. I didn't want to wreck lives but it was difficult to make a clean break – it lingered on and off for far too long. I've not been with another man since, so like you, that's a long time too."

"You don't see him now?"

"He's a very senior executive now. I see him occasionally in the course of my work and we are friends. It's not a problem. But as I said I've not had a relationship with him at all for several years. Prior to that I had a relationship at university – of sorts. From day one I was pestered from the subtle to the blatant. It wouldn't stop so I made the best looking one of them, who also happened to command respect from the other guys, my supposed boyfriend and the others left me alone. I didn't love him. It was more like a working arrangement if you see what I mean."

God, she was stunning and I didn't doubt that there were always men after her. But I believed her when she said she wasn't responsive to that. She had depth and was mature for her years and I could well understand her affair with an older man. I imagined her having a preference for older company in general. Her looks could easily give the wrong impression but in my experience I have often found just the reverse – that the least attractive can be looser in their ways. I leaned to her. "Thanks for talking to me too."

She kissed her fingers and put them to my cheek. "Shall we have some food?" she asked. "I suggest we have just a little now and a drink. Not too much because we don't want that long swim on a full stomach although it will be a while before we start back. A little will give us some energy and besides, we must eat together on our own little island."

"I agree with every word you say," I told her. "I like the way you refer to this as *our* little island."

"Well it is isn't it? When was the last person here? Maybe never. Maybe we have claimed it? What do you think?"

"I think you're absolutely right. Maybe we should name it and declare UDI. A unilateral declaration of independence and plant our own flag on it. I could draw up the paperwork! But it's your island really – you discovered it."

"But I wanted to share it with you. I wouldn't bring anyone else here."

"Thanks," I told her as I put my hand round her shoulder and pulled her head to mine. Thanks for sharing it with me."

The lunch was a selection of small filo pastries with vegetables inside with some exquisite dips and canned sparkling mineral water. "Real surfers drink straight from the can," I was told, which was her subtle way of explaining that she hadn't brought glasses. "Even James Bond drinks from the can nowadays. I have seen it!"

"Well that's alright then."

She took out her cigarettes from the bag and as was becoming customary, I lit one for her. "Would you like one or will you share mine?" she asked.

"Maybe I'll just have a few puffs of yours," I said. "So is it a continual problem – being touched, being approached?" I asked.

"In a word, yes! Not every flight but it's never far away. When I'm walking down the aisle I see many of the men looking at me but most are not making eye contact, they are watching my body – undressing me in their mind. When their eyes finally turn up to mine I simply give them a tight lipped smile and move on. You are not most men Matt but would you undress an air hostess with your eyes?"

"You're full of loaded questions," I told her.

"I'm interested to know," said she, looking at me endearingly.

"I don't have to," I told her. "I just take a long, long walk along the beach to a very remote cove and hey presto! My imagination is not needed."

She laughed, "I'm definitely going to rough you up, Matt!" she said looking me straight in the face.

"Is it a problem on the charter flights too?"

"Can be – that's just different. Proposals for dinner in the evening, even proposals of marriage simply after a flight. One guy really annoyed me though. I was on a private charter from Rome to Athens and he asked me to have dinner with him at his hotel. He had a suite there apparently. I thanked him but said I was very sorry but I'm not available. He then asked me if I knew who he was. He told me he was in a position to influence my career – one way or the other – as he put it and suggested I might like to become available. I asked him if he was seriously suggesting that he would use his influence to my detriment if I refused him. His face simply gave an expression to suggest 'your choice.' I felt absolute disgust. I looked at him hard. I looked into the face of that rich grubby obnoxious little twat."

"Oh, I want him," I said, feeling the same disgust.

"Too late!" said she. "He made his move when we were getting ready to disembark. I knew that a very senior executive of the airline was on the tarmac outside – a senior executive that I know *very* well! – so I called him on my mobile phone and told him what had happened while this guy listened. The very senior executive came up into the plane immediately and confronted him. He denied it, saying it was all a misunderstanding. But I was always going to be believed and anyway my assistant on the flight heard every word of it and delighted in confirming what she heard. He was made to apologise to me and then he was told he wouldn't be welcome on any future flights with the airline. He was on a loser in this day and age."

"Wonderful!"

Elena became a little emotional as she said, "I hated that. He threatens people's careers to get what he wants. The bastard! I can handle myself but what about the younger girls?"

I touched her arm. "Good for you Elena – good for you!"

"On the normal flights it's as you might expect – less subtle! The mile high club, I fancy you, can you help me… One guy even told me he fancied a bit of Greek. I told him that when he is in Athens he should contact an escort agency, I was sure they would help but he should expect to pay dearly for the privilege."

"And the pilots or other crew?"

"They're ok. They've given up," said she expressing satisfaction. "They protect me from the new guys now– they're warned off at the outset,"

"Does the airline have procedures for dealing with those sort of issues?"

"Guidelines but it's left very much to our discretion. It's often easier to smile and ignore or just give a polite no – not to make an issue out of something that by the occasion is often out of character and of the moment. There was however one chap who was part of a rugby team on their way to a game. You know, one of eleven silly buggers who chase bags of wind," she said, laughing. "I was standing in the aisle bending towards to a passenger in the window seat on the opposite side when one of the team got up from behind me, put his hands on my waist as he pretended it was difficult for him to squeeze by me, which it wasn't. As his hands steadied me he brushed hard against me as he slid by and was quite clearly aroused." She put her mouth to my ear and whispered, "He had an erection." I'm not surprised I thought but kept quiet! "He then went on to the toilet at the back of the plane. When he came back and re-seated himself, I put my face to his and I told him with deadly precision, 'So now in your most private of moments you will be able to bring me to mind as if it was a real event but you touch me again and I'll have security waiting for you when we land.'"

"I think you're amazing," I told her, "truly." She looked at me and we laughed together. "I've told you that you should need a licence to wear that uniform."

Elena explained that the dress code for in-flight duty was very strict. Obviously the uniform must be worn and exactly as specified. But bras must be worn and of a type that is fully supportive and shows no more than a general outline – no movement or details. The legs must be covered with tights or stockings in the thickness and colour laid down but if stockings are worn, there must be no hint of suspenders through the skirt." I obviously looked pensive for a few moments.

"What are you thinking?"

I came back to the moment. "No… I can't go there," I said with conviction.

"Ahh…" said she expressing her disappointment. I share with you my secret island that I've never shared with anyone else and you won't share your thoughts with me."

"Oh– I'm sorry! It's a beautiful island, it really is. Quite amazing actually and I'm very appreciative that you choose to share it with me."

"That is not what you were thinking Matt Rochester and you know it!" She adopted a more serious tone. "Objection your honour, hotshot lawyer seeks to deflect matters by withholding the truth." She changed her voice again and said, "Sustained! Council should recognise the sincerity of the moment and share his thoughts truthfully," and she looked hard at me with demanding eyes at the same time she was obviously holding back a huge grin.

I looked into her. "Do you really want to know what I was thinking when you were telling me about the dress code?"

"Yes," said she determinedly. And then she changed her tone to one of softness, "Please – share it with me. I want to know."

"You might be shocked."

"I've been around in this world long enough not to be shocked by men's thoughts"

"Really!"

"Yes."

Well, there are men's thoughts and then there are men's thoughts," I told her, "and as I have said, my thoughts and imagination have intensified with abstinence for a long period of time."

"All the more interesting." She was not going to be deterred and in an affectionate voice said, "I'm waiting."

"Oh, very well. Just between you and me."

She looked around. "I don't see anyone else."

I beckoned her closer and she put her head close to mine in 'let's share a secret' mode. "I've seen you in your uniform and you look … well, provocative enough." Her face was intense. What was I going to say? "But a soft bra with your firm walk in a fine blouse and the outline of a suspender belt under your tight skirt walking up the aisle of the plane. 'Well, members of the jury, my client was unable to settle into the flight as he would wish. He was veritably induced to think provocatively. It was more like a raunchy night club act than aircraft hospitality. I plead he was induced to express himself in a way that in ordinary circumstances might seem untoward. In short, his mind was blown.'"

"There! That wasn't difficult was it? Many men would imagine a similar scenario but I wouldn't be walking down the aisle of an aeroplane and I wouldn't be wearing a skirt or a blouse."

"Well to truthfully answer your earlier question, whilst not being most men, I too wouldn't be averse to undressing an air hostess in uniform with my eyes, or probably women in other circumstances if they presented in a certain way."

"Is that right?"

"Absolutely! And, you're getting the censored version of events anyway"

"A psychiatrist might say you are not clearing the bottlenecks if you're censoring your output."

"That psychiatrist might have cleared some bottlenecks but ruined some beautiful friendships simultaneously."

"Have another spinach and feta parcel," I was told.

"Do you know," I said, "Here we are sitting together on the remotest of little islands gazing out to infinity and we've had filo parcels with dips, talked not only of past relationships but of impropriety on aircraft, our types of swimwear or the absence of it, through to soft bras and suspender belts and all of it whilst sharing a black Indonesian cigarette."

She put her arm round me and rocked us from side to side as we both laughed. "And I've loved it," she said.

"Me too."

And that's how it was. That's how it always was with Elena – spontaneous, uninhibited, informative and great fun. The swim back seemed to take an eternity. I could be forgiven for thinking a tide or current was against us but I knew that it was no more than that for some reason, a return journey always seems longer. And also because the conversation and the laughter and the deep water splashing fight come roughhouse, didn't give way to purposeful swimming until we realised that it needed more purpose if we were to get back the same day!

Chapter 13

"I won," said Elena with authority but stifling a laugh.

"No, I won."

"Don't be so silly, Matt. I won!"

"You're living in a make belief world," I told her.

"Look, if a handicap had been applied to allow for your superior height and strength, I would have won hands down."

"If, would have – wishful thinking doesn't come into it."

"Anyway, you're ticklish – very ticklish Matt Rochester and I was about to press that home to advantage."

"About to! Was that before or while you were in an arm lock?"

"I was summoning determination – mind over matter. And with more time I would have triumphed."

"About to, would have, more time. It seems you were almost but not quite on a roll. How much time did you need?" She laughed openly, our heads engaging

Our conversation over dinner in the taverna was animated and punctuated by laughter, either expressed or stifled in a bid to profess a seriousness to things. Having washed her hair and made up, and particularly around her eyes, Elena presented as a mature sophisticated and very Greek woman, but our interaction was still as it was on that remote island. The transition from wild in a bikini to sophisticated in a blouse and skirt didn't override our rapport.

"So what form would this handicap take – a thirty second start maybe?"

"No, one arm behind your back."

"In deep water!"

"You can handle yourself."

"Look! – I'd been nailed to the wall, I'd had my life history extracted, my soul bared, private thoughts prised into the open and I was threatened with roughing up, not once but twice. Reprisals were inevitable. You needed sorting and a deliberate splash from you halfway back from the island was the trigger. Even with one arm behind my back life at that moment would have been difficult for you."

Did she laugh! "Is that right?" We'll test that theory another…"

We were interrupted and with our foreheads almost touching we both turned to see that Jennifer had approached our table.

"Hi Elena, Matt."

"Jennifer. You're back," I said in my surprise, stating the obvious. I saw Stefanos sitting at a table not far away and guessed she had just come in and detoured to us before joining him. He gestured in acknowledgement in his laid-back way. It was more of a peace symbol. "I didn't see you come in."

"I'm not surprised. You two have been locked in head to head combat. Am I disturbing the fun or is it a timely intervention?"

We all three laughed. "Oh this is purely verbal," said Elena, "nothing like the physical combat in deep water that we had earlier. I was just explaining to Matt that it was me who won."

Jennifer laughed openly again. "Oh wonderful," she said,

"So how was the UK?" I asked.

"Same as always. I'm happier on the plane coming back than when I'm going but it served its purpose. I got some things done. Now it's back to the business of enjoying life. Take care you two," said she, putting her hand up to us as she returned to her table.

Stefanos stood up as Jennifer reached their table – a very respectful form of acknowledgement. She touched the side of his face with her hand and held it there for a while with an endearing smile before they sat down opposite one another. Both Elena and I saw it and it was all so telling – the greeting, dining together in the evening immediately upon her return and her disposition. To some extent we were seeing what Alex had seen but whereas he was reading between the lines, we were seeing the scenario in play in real-time. We looked at each other and spontaneously smiled.

"With non-attachment would you think?" asked Elena.

I nodded. "I would think so."

"Do you know, I think it's quite beautiful and I'm so pleased for them," said Elena. But where she had only her mind's eye to assess things, I of course had seen one of their most personal moments and as a consequence, I would add the word powerful to Elena's beautiful, as for a brief moment I relived what I had seen. "You look pensive," she said.

"I agree with you completely," I replied, coming back to the moment. "Unusual and very beautiful," I added, before Elena put a chip in my mouth to signal the re-commencement of our meal.

"Matt. I have to go back to the airline tomorrow for two or possibly three days."

"I thought you said you had some time off."

"Yes, I did but the girl who was doing a charter flight from Athens to Dubai is sick and they've asked me if I will do it. They are VIP customers and I must step up. I'm sorry, I wanted us to be together for a while," said she, touching my hand lightly. "I didn't want to say earlier and spoil the evening."

"Needs must. I know you're very important to the airline. Yes, I'm disappointed but I'll look forward to your return. I saw a dance advertised at a venue in the mountains – Karditsa is it? I saw a picture of it on a poster. It looked like an old ruin."

"Oh that would be…" and she gave me a Greek name which was unpronounceable to me. "It's a big event and draws people from afar. It's held every year, sometimes twice."

"I'm told it's very popular, do you go?"

"I have been a few times but I wouldn't go on my own. Greek men… they expect too much."

"Is it good? The venue looked interesting."

"Yes it is good. Very large, lots of people. An old ruin in the mountains, partly outdoors, partly in and they have live bands – Greek and international dance. It's very atmospheric."

"Would you like to go with me?"

Her face lit up. "Yes. Oh yes, I'd love to go with you Matt. What are the dates?"

I gave her the dates and she took her diary from her bag to check. It was almost two weeks away. "Yes I'm not on duty then," she said, beaming at me and she wrote it in. "Lovely, we can look forward to that," she added touching my arm.

"Is the food good? They're offering some tables for early booking."

"It's ok. Yes, let's have a table."

"I'll book one on line," I said with enthusiasm. She was clearly delighted and squeezed my arm gently.

"Coffee and brandy outside?" she asked when the food was finished and we seated ourselves at the little table under the lantern. The drinks poured, she took out her cigarettes and put her lighter on the table. She liked me to light it for her as she leaned closer across the table. "This is my second cigarette today," said she, referring to the one we shared on the island. Some days I don't smoke. I don't usually smoke when I'm working. I appreciate them more that way. I smoke for pleasure at special moments not out of habit or addiction."

"You're disciplined – I think in your life generally. You've got it together."

"Thanks Matt. I work on it!" "I think the proportion of people in Greece who smoke is higher than in many other countries."

"Why do think that is?"

"I don't know. Maybe it's the stress of keeping all that passion under control," said she, her profound sense of humour never far away. Then she said in softened tones, "I really loved today Matt – It will stay with me while I'm away." And then touching my arm she added, "I'm so sorry I have to go tomorrow."

"Me too," I said expressing my sadness, "but your career is important, obviously. I'll get stuck into my writing – it's starting to shape. Maybe we can keep in touch and do something together on your return. Pick up where we left off."

"Of course! Of course we will!"

And I too would relive the day, many times in fact and starting when I returned to my room. A recognition that it was all so real – not some imagined scenario. That mature, highly attractive and immaculately presented woman that I first saw at the bottom of the stairs in the taverna, now had a name. And more! She had a presence – a presence that I sensed on first sight but have now experienced for real and progressively so. From our first words together in the bar, we had an instant rapport. I have a vivid imagination but even my wildest dreams wouldn't have dared to envisage such a scenario. I felt very privileged.

And I would tell those male passengers of hers, straining their imagination to experience more than cabin service from her, that I have spent time with her, laughed with her and talked with her at great length and depth and of many things from the sublime to the preposterous and then some. We have shared brandies together under the old lantern in the night air. I have been intimate with her, not by way of physical sex but by intercourse of a different nature. Of a rapport spontaneous and unfettered, allowed to run free, with self-expression allowing intimate exchange of ones thoughts. I would tell them that we drove to a very remote area and swam together to a secret island offshore and spent time there so alone that the intimacy was almost tangible. She wore a bikini, I would say, not of the 'Is she wearing one or not' variety, although she informed that she had those too, but one fit for wild swimming – every inch as alluring, fitting to perfection and exuding sheer class. I would take them to the edge of their comprehension by telling them of the horseplay in the sea – a roughhouse that only two strong swimmers could have survived. For I had spent time with the real Elena and shared a depth and fun that imaginations would be pushed to envisage. Even their stretched imaginations couldn't conjure what was my reality. To be in my shoes, the proverbial loss of their right arm may well be a consideration too far but they would surely be eating their hearts out.

And I asked myself why we hadn't had sex. An onlooker would have surely seen it as inevitable, perhaps assumed that we were already in a relationship and that in itself is another story. But that roughhouse in the sea was in fact making love in all but name. It was a release of sexual tension in the absence of physical love. And when we finally reached the mainland beach, I took her hand to steady her as we walked over the unevenness of the sand and the stones back to her jeep. Even in the absence of her high heels I was aware of her unusual and alluring walk which by her body movement transmitted through her hands. We communicated through those hands, a reassurance with spent emotions and it signified a togetherness after our shared experience. And what I felt was the same that I would have felt if we had made love. We dried ourselves off and dressed, not overtly or without care but with less reserve than would have been exercised previously. Eye contact brought a mutual smile with unspoken words – we had a humbling sense of reverence. The closeness and intimacy of the day made the antics in the sea almost inevitable as a release and our later reaction to one-another was surely the same as if we had made love. Yes, I too would relive the day and cherish it.

Chapter 14

Elena was away, keeping in touch by texting, Jennifer was back and good for brief chats.

I got stuck into my writing. I had a framework and copious notes and I enjoyed trying to bring the early stages of the story together. In my room, on the beach or seated outside a taverna in a small mountain village, my writing folder was always with me. A few days on my own was very useful and in honesty very productive. Elena was inspirational and I certainly missed her company but when we were together the conversation never stopped and I needed solitude to start putting things together.

I chatted to Jennifer every day and that was nice. She was a lovely person and good to talk to. Stefanos was around and we too had the occasional chat with no shortage of subjects – Eastern philosophy, Harley Davidsons, surfing and villa restoration were always on the agenda with goats and cats a possibility should that be required. I really did like the guy. He lived in a different world but one that was very real and meaningful to him and one that I could relate to.

It was on the day of Elena's return after three day's absence that the lingering smoke from my portending candle made its ominous presence felt once more. We were sitting at an outside table of the taverna catching up with a drink when Jennifer came up and asked if she could join us, seeming to have something on her mind.

"Of course Jennifer," I told her and she pulled up a chair from the neighbouring table.

"Hi Elena, are you ok? Good trip?" she asked.

"Yes, thanks Jennifer."

"Look," said Jennifer, "are you guys aware of the Englishman that's putting himself around in the village?"

Elena looked puzzled and shook her head. She was unaware having been away. "I think I know who you mean," I said, having seen this guy to whom she was referring. He stood out being one of the few if not the only obvious English person around at the present time apart from myself.

"He's cropping up everywhere," said Jennifer. "I see him virtually every time I look up – in the village, in the taverna, on the beach, and even around the area of my villa. I could be forgiven for thinking he might be stalking me. He's strange, he's not like the average tourist. He seems to be more interested in what other people are doing rather than having a purpose of his own. He gives me the creeps."

"Yes, he looks on the strange side and as you say, he doesn't seem to fit usual scenarios. Is he staying in the village do you know?"

"Someone told me he's staying at a house at the end of the village, just off on the right," said Jennifer but not sounding too sure of the exact location.

"That sounds like Aliki's place. She has a couple of rooms she lets out," said Elena.

"Do you know her?" I asked.

"Yes very well," said Elena with conviction. "When we get an enquiry for a room and we are fully booked, we will refer them to Aliki and vice versa."

I had my suspicions even before Jennifer mentioned him. "If he's snooping around I think we should try and find out. Would it be possible to find anything out about him from your friend, do you think?" I asked Elena. "Anything! But even his name and where he's from would be helpful. I have a source. I could look into it – probably add substance to our curiosity."

"Mm," said Elena, "I'll give her a ring. I'll do it now – why not?" She took her phone from her bag and scrolled through. "I don't seem to have her number here. Excuse me," she said as she stood up and walked into the taverna to get the number and make the call.

"How's the writing coming along," asked Jennifer. "Is it working for you here?"

"It's definitely working for me here," I told her, "Writing or not. I love this part of Greece and this taverna is amazing – it's very foreign but it feels like home. The cuisine, the sea, the climate, the mountain villages, it all suits me well."

"And you have friends in Elena and Stefanos which must have helped you to settle in."

"Yes, I feel very fortunate to have their friendship and yours Jennifer. I value your friendship and yes I'm getting into the writing – I'm sure it will work for me."

"And I yours Matt," said she canting her head slightly with a soft smile. "Your book – is it a novel?"

"A fact based novel on my experiences to start with. I like to write on philosophical matters so building that into a story is one way of doing it. I'll see how it goes."

Elena came back with a purposeful walk and an expression on her face to suggest mission accomplished. Sitting back down at the table she put a piece of paper in front of me on which was written this guy's full name and date of birth. "And he lives in London," said Elena. "Aliki has his passport. I haven't got any more but she says he's a bit strange. Nice enough in the scheme of things but not easy going. Doesn't talk much at all. He seems secretive, not like the average tourist or business traveller. Asks a lot of questions about the village and doesn't seem to be interested in travelling around. He's told Aliki he's here for a while to unwind. Other than that, that's all that's known. Maybe he's just a weirdo!"

"Thanks Elena. I'll put that to my source, see if I can find anything of interest."

"Thanks Matt," said Jennifer, appreciative that it was being looked into. She definitely felt uncomfortable about him and I knew how she felt. From what I had seen, it wasn't difficult to see the guy as a stalker.

Elena and I spent the day together. A walk along the beach, a swim and then a drive into the mountains for a late lunch.

"So you're getting some writing done," she said. "A title yet?"

"No, not yet but I'm getting into it."

"So tell me, in your fact based story with disguised characters what's my fictional name?"

"Daisy," I told her.

She laughed spontaneously and then looking into me she said with contrived menace, "Be very careful!" Fun as always but we had our deeper moments too.

"Tell me about some of your court work, Matt," she asked. "If you're able to that is. From what you have said, you were disillusioned or frustrated. You'd had enough. Was it one case or one particular aspect?" She looked into me deeply. She was not making topical conversation. She sensed there was something that defined my decision and was eager to engage.

"No, not one particular case but yes, a particular aspect. I suppose it was something that built with time and simply came to a head. I entered the legal profession as a free spirit but there is a framework, a code of practice, a set of rules to which one must conform and to a great extent I accepted that had to be and whilst it didn't always sit easily, I was a free spirit contained – not a rebel. Most entrants followed the rules implicitly. They play the game, as it were.

"So I'm good with words. I've always been good with words. I was told at university I was good with words. I'm told in court that I'm good with words. And I win cases because I'm good with words. A jury has come to a verdict largely because of my words. Some have been sentenced or freed largely because of my words but are they guilty or innocent?" Elena looked deeper into me.

"In my early days I was in debating societies. It was a big thing for me. I took part in so many debates and travelled widely to do so. Very often on given subjects we were appointed to speak either for or against the motion – not given a choice. On one occasion I won the debate speaking *for* the motion and the next day I won again speaking *against* the same motion. The plaudits rained on me. From tutors to opponents – from well done to bloody clever old chap. I was good with words wasn't I! But what does that mean for the subject we were debating? Nothing, is the short answer. All it means is that I was able to put forward an argument and destroy the opposing argument to win the day. But in reality, I've probably not proved or disproved the motion itself. So as far as the proposal is concerned everyone is none the wiser in the deeper context. If it was a court case I would have enabled a guilty verdict one day and a not guilty verdict on the same case the next day and the defendant would have been judged accordingly. But is he guilty or not guilty? It doesn't prove beyond reasonable doubt. All it proves is that I'm good with words. I win debates. And we play the game. We play by the rules. One lawyer does his best to make the defendant guilty and another lawyer does his best to make him innocent and the jury decides. People come up to me afterwards in court –

'Congratulations!' 'Bravo!' But I'm not debating in some society, I'm hugely influential in life changing situations and I don't want the accused found guilty or not because I'm good with words. Sometimes I don't like my words. Sometimes I hate myself. Sometimes I don't like to hear myself speak. Once out of the courtroom I untie my hair and become the person that I am, not the person I have to be. I'm no longer playing the game and with reflection I often feel uneasy."

Elena leaned closer and put her hand on my arm.

"I feel most uneasy in cases where there is no strong or direct evidence where it's one person's word against another and the case rests purely on debate. There are guidelines on making a case without evidence. Think about that! Without evidence it's purely probabilities, purely debate. Being clever with words. So the jury will base their decision on the debate that they have heard. So on one day I could have someone found guilty and the next day found innocent, depending on my brief.

"I want to use my mind and my words to find and express a greater truth. I seek a scenario where I don't have to listen to my own words. I seek a scenario where I may find a higher truth without the need for my words however good they might be. A scenario where I listen and not speak."

Elena continued looking into me deeply – motionless for some moments. Then she pulled up her chair to mine and she embraced me putting her head to the side of mine. She hugged me tightly and I could sense her emotions. When she eventually released me, I looked into her face and her eyes were moist with tears.

"Hey," I whispered

"Hey," she responded, showing a reserved smile.

"So," I said in summary. "I need to find myself. I need to find meaning – a greater reality. A reality that Stefanos has already experienced to a greater extent. A West Country beach with a surf board was right for me in my youth but now it is not the answer. Alone on a yacht in the southern ocean might be but that, certainly at the moment, would be a bit drastic. I'm not looking to drop right out, so long walks on sandy beaches and time in remote coves is the current alternative."

"And a taverna in remote Greece," said Elena.

"And a very special taverna in remote Greece."

"Thank you for talking to me Matt. Thanks for talking to me," she repeated in a softer tone, with tears still apparent in her eyes, as she hugged me yet again running her hand through my hair.

When we parted I looked to her and I said "Thank *you*! Thank you for listening, for giving me the opportunity to speak."

"You need to Matt. Any time. You can talk to me anytime – you know that! I understand!"

We were brought back to the moment by my phone signalling an incoming message. It was my source. I opened it and was not surprised at what I read. I showed it to Elena:

Subject is private detective based London. Sole operator and not registered.

Elena drew a breath and held her mouth open, aghast.

"I must let Jennifer know immediately," I said. Elena raised her eyebrows. "Well I don't think he's watching you or me."

I sent a message to Jennifer: *Stalker is London based private detective. That's all I have, really but will talk later if you wish.*

And it *was* Jennifer's wish. That evening, she came up to me as I was sitting at the bar in the taverna talking to Elena prior to finding a table for dinner. She came straight to me.

"Hello Matt," she said, obviously pleased that I was there to talk to. She gave Elena a lovely smile but her focus was to me. "Have you got a few minutes?"

I stood. "Yes – yes of course I have. Shall we go over to that table," I said, gesturing to one of the small tables by the wall. "Can I get you a drink?"

"Oh, let me get you one," Jennifer said.

"No, I'm fine thanks. I don't normally drink before dinner. I enjoy a glass of wine with my meal and perhaps a little brandy after and I discipline myself to that. I'm no drinker really but you have one – please."

She smiled and said, "A gin and tonic would be nice," with an intonation that suggested it was needed. Elena heard what was said, looked at me and I nodded.

"I'll bring it over to you," she said, giving me an understanding look.

"Thank you for your message Matt," said Jennifer as we sat down. "Thank you for finding out. There must be some costs incurred and I will of course pay."

I put my hand on hers briefly and assured her there were no costs involved. "I have a source and it's a two way thing and this would be just a few minutes work."

Elena came and discretely put a gin and tonic in front of Jennifer, not wanting to disturb us and she lightly touched my shoulder as she turned away.

"I think he must be working for my husband. We are estranged. As you are aware I spend most of my time here now and I think that's likely to continue. I think he's probably anxious to know if I have someone else in my life – having an affair or even living with someone. Maybe he was suspicious when I bought the villa. But there wasn't anyone. It was just that I wanted a different life and preferably one in the sun. I love Greece and when I was out here, I saw this villa was for sale. I fell in love with it and its location – this whole area really and I put in an offer. There was no-one else. I met Stefan here and in talking to him I realised he was just the man to help with its renovation. He's a lovely man and... well... I'm worried that this detective may tell my husband that it's more than a working relationship."

"Mm. it's a pity we didn't know about him earlier. He's obviously been snooping around for a few days now – long enough to get the picture and formulate a viewpoint."

"Can he be trusted do you think?"

"I think he can be trusted to earn his fee. How accurate his telling of events is, is down to him. One other thing I am told is that he is not registered with the recognised bodies that govern private detectives."

"Doesn't he have to be?"

"No. he can operate as a detective purely on his practical experience but what it does mean is that he is not bound by the code of practice of a governing body that a registered one would be. He obviously has to be careful what he's doing for his own sake but subject to that he would be a law unto himself. He will not necessarily be operating within a framework that's laid down. That doesn't mean that he's unscrupulous, just that he has more scope to be so, should he be that way inclined. But I know nothing about him or his reputation so one must reserve judgement."

"So he could say all sorts of things to justify a fee."

"Yes, but I wouldn't expect him to fabricate stories and they usually back up their reports with photographs." Jennifer flinched when I uttered the word photographs. "There are, however, different ways they can present facts."

"Bugger," said Jennifer, half under her breath.

"Look! We don't know what his brief is and there is the old saying of not worrying about things you cannot change. You are now aware and have some time to consider possible scenarios should events turn as you may suspect. Worry about it then and if you want to chat further, you know I'm around."

"Thanks Matt. Thanks a lot," she reiterated touching my arm as we stood up, adding "It's good to have you to talk to."

I went back to Elena at the bar and she gave me a look of resignation. "She's worried, isn't she?"

"Yes, I don't know the full set-up with her husband – only that they are estranged."

I knew that Alex would be interested to see if I featured in Jennifer's life but I had no concerns in that regard. This detective would have seen that I spent my time with Elena but it would of course be obvious who Jennifer spent most of her time with and I felt sure he would have photographs to back his report.

Chapter 15

Elena was to go back on duty today but we had breakfast together in the taverna before she left. Another sad parting but it's that sadness that confirmed how beautiful our friendship was.

It was as I returned to the taverna having helped Elena with her bags to her car that I saw Jennifer sitting at a table outside. She looked wrong! Sitting outside was unusual for her for breakfast and she didn't cut her usual posture. There was an air of dejection about her. I walked over to her but she didn't seem to notice. She was within herself – pre-occupied and there was a coffee in front of her that hadn't been started.

"Hey," I said with a soft friendly intonation. "Are you ok?"

"Hey," she acknowledged as she looked up but didn't answer my question. And as she looked at me I could see great sadness in her eyes and within seconds, tears came, her lips puckered tightly and she tried in vain to hold back a crying from within.

I pulled a chair closer to her and sat down. "Can I help? Would you like to talk?" I said. She stared at her coffee but seemingly without focus, her lips quivering where words wouldn't form. "Tell me," I said softly, entreating her as I touched her arm on the table.

She turned to me and with difficulty said, "My husband is going to out Stefan," and her crying broke out, visibly and audibly. A friendly approach was the trigger for her release. "He's given me an ultimatum."

The ill wind that I had sensed from beyond the horizon made its presence felt. It had arrived and the smoke from my candle was swirling and had turned acrid.

I held her arm. "Would you like to talk? Go through it together?"

"I'd like that if it's alright with you?"

"Of course it is! Let's start with some fresh coffee," I said, catching the attention of the waitress.

"So first things, first. You've heard from your husband. What did he say?"

"He wants me to stop my relationship with Stefan immediately or he's going to make known the problems he has had in the past." She put her head closer to mine and in a softer voice said, "I think he had drug problems in the Far East before he went into the monastery but I don't know the full details."

"So this is the result of the private detective – the stalker from Hell!"

"Yes, my husband's got a report from him and with photographs."

I winced to myself. What would these photos show – holding hands, kissing, or fearfully, had the detective seen what I had seen? "Didn't waste much time did he and neither has your husband. Has he said what's in the photos?"

"No. No he hasn't."

A pot of coffee was put on the table with fresh cups and Jennifer's original one, now cold, taken away.

"Do you know how he found out about Stefan's past? Unless there was widespread publicity, these things are not so easy to find, particularly in retrospect."

"No, I don't."

"Is there anyone from around here who knows of his past?"

"I'm not sure. I think some people might know he had a troubled time but whether they know the detail, I don't know."

"I can't help thinking that it would be someone locally that's given information to the detective rather than information obtained from the Far East in which case, so called outing him might not be the sensation that your husband has in mind."

"I see what you mean, but there's more. My husband is threatening to make it known to all my contacts in England, that I am having an affair with a goat herder. This would include my media contacts, publishers and most importantly the TV companies. I have done television work. If he does, the press will pick it up and have a field day won't they? You know, well-known lady about town has affair with hippy Greek goat herder with a past, the details of which would then come out. My life would never be the same again and neither would Stefan's. There would be reporters and photographers here and whatever they pick up would be embellished. His peaceful retreat would be shattered."

"But there's more than the publicity – the outing aspect. In my marriage, there is a pre-nuptial agreement. It's complex – I can't go into details. My husband will inherit considerable wealth, which in itself is subject to caveats – hence the complex prenup. It specifies relationships apart from much else."

My mind was in overdrive. Was my being headhunted for Jennifer a setup, part of a scheme for Alex to profit from a known affair, or enable a divorce on his terms? If it was, it didn't work but it would seem that an affair with Stefan has struck a discordant note. Or has it in some way played into Alex's hands and he's making maximum capital out of it. I recall Alex telling me that he was estranged but that divorce was not an option. That neither of them had expressed a wish in that regard, saying there are private reasons why that is not likely to happen. Without the detail of the prenup I wouldn't know, but to ruin people's lives by virtual blackmail of their past is anathema to me. It could be said that Jennifer is a victim of her own indiscretion but in these circumstances I did feel sorry for her as the person I have come to know. But so far as Stefanos is concerned I found it particularly objectionable. Yes, he was obviously having a relationship with a married woman but she is estranged and in a faraway place and it does take two to make a bargain. He doesn't deserve his distant past to catch up with him and prejudice his present peace and contentment. There was probably more to it but I felt sorry for both Stefan and Jennifer and as a friend to both, I was prepared to help and I believed I had the means.

"Mm, it's blackmail. A lot of people have a past from which they've moved on – got a new life, and I don't like people that find out things and threaten their new life. I find it abhorrent! I'd like to help if I can. Do you know of anything untoward in your husband's past?"

Jennifer closed her eyes and shook her head. "No – not that I know of."

"Look, I know your husband."

"You know Alex?" She looked very thoughtful. "Did he send you here to spy on me?"

"No, no. no! If he did, he wouldn't need a private detective would he? He headhunted me some time ago for some prestigious clients that he had in the UK. It was mainly contracts and legal advice but when he offered further work, I told him of my plans for a new life. At the time I was actively looking at the Greek islands. He told me of this place, thinking it matched my criteria pretty well. I researched it and it seemed ideal. Not the islands but offering me the escape in surroundings that I was looking for and with this Taverna as the ideal place for me to stay away from tourism generally. He then mentioned that you and he were estranged and that you were renovating a villa here. That's how he knew of this place. He knows I found you attractive because I told him so in passing – I'd seen you with him briefly on two occasions."

Jennifer looked at me out of the top of her eyes, with her head down. "You didn't come on to me," she said, to draw my response.

"I didn't come here for that reason. And wouldn't have done for any aspect in that regard but from what you say, I'm beginning to see that I may have been head-hunted for reasons I wasn't to know."

"Yes – interesting."

"Look, Jennifer, I think I may well be able to help and with what I know now, I would like to step up. I don't want knowledge of your marital arrangements – I won't get involved in that. But as I have said, the blackmail aspect appals me and if I can help with that, then that in itself may resolve some if not all of your prenup concerns. I was planning a trip to London very shortly but I will bring that forward. I will reschedule my meetings and go as soon as I can arrange a flight. I would like to meet with Alex." I leaned to her and held her arm as I said "Bear with me. I need a few days but in the meantime don't worry about it. Ok?"

"Thanks Matt," she said, giving me a reserved smile.

"That's better. Have you told Stefan?"

"No, this has only just come in," she replied gesturing with her phone. "Do you think I should?"

"I think he ought to be made aware of what is happening, particularly if that detective is still hanging around but similarly tell him not to worry at the moment."

"Mm. Yes you're right."

"I had no understanding with Alex and certainly no obligation. I see this as my new life and the friendship of Stefan, you, and Elena are very important to me."

Jennifer came closer and turned her head into mine. "I'm so pleased to see you and her together. She's amazing! She could loosen you up somewhat."

That amused me. "Do I look as though I need loosening up – somewhat?"

"You look great to me but to the observant eye, Elena could be just the person to make your slotting into this new life, a perfect fit."

"Are you matchmaking?"

She smiled, "Yes, I think I might be."

I leaned to her. "Right! You of course, have already been loosened up and it shows – to the observant eye, that is – which is, basically, why your husband is on a war footing!!"

She laughed! "Oh I'd love to hear you in court, Matt."

I stood up and held out my hand and as she took it I said, "Friends?"

"Friends!" she said as she continued to hold my hand for a few moments adding "I'm very grateful for your help Matt."

"You've got it," I said as I walked away but she called me back.

"Matt." I turned back to her. "Thank you for being honest with me!"

I nodded. "If there are sides to be taken, I'm on yours!"

I sat down again at her table, took out my phone and said "Bear with me a moment," and I compiled the following text:

Alex, I know of your latest communication with Jennifer. Imperative you do nothing before we speak!! I'm rescheduling my planned visit to London and will come as soon as I can arrange flight. Matt.

I held my phone towards Jennifer for her to read it. "Are you ok with me sending that?" I asked her.

She gave me an appreciative smile and said, "Yes."

"The alternative is to capitulate and give in to his demands but even if you do that, it may not end there. He will always potentially have one over on you – a hand he could play at any time."

"The sword of Damocles," said a thoughtful Jennifer.

"Exactly!"

I sent the message.

Chapter 16

I rescheduled my meetings and got a flight from Thessaloniki to London the day after next. Alex was making time for me and I sent a message to Elena to let her know what was happening:

Hi, the detective has made his report and Jennifer and Stefanos are under threat of exposure by an ultimatum. I'm appalled and brought forward London visit to meet Jennifer's husband. I fly 15ᵗʰ X

Elena and I were texting each other every day now, which together with signing off with a kiss was a sign of our closeness. She replied immediately:

Hi, How awful!!! They must be very pleased to have your help! I'm flying into Heathrow on 18ᵗʰ with few hours turnaround. Any chance you will still be there? Could we possibly meet? X

I was ecstatic! I was due to fly back on the 18ᵗʰ but I would extend it a day to meet Elena. She was on a long spell of duty so to see her earlier than expected would be wonderful. Plus the fact after two meetings with clients and a confrontation with Alex, to have a possible dinner with Elena before I returned would give my trip greater meaning.

Wonderful! Will delay return to see you on 18ᵗʰ give me times and I will meet you at Heathrow. X

I met with my clients, leaving the 17ᵗʰ free to see Alex. It seemed somewhat strange having meetings on legal matters in London again but it was a nice strange – not nostalgic. I experienced it as a visitor from my new life, not as a return from holiday and if I wasn't seeing Elena, like Jennifer had said, I would be longing for the return flight. I did however have the meeting with Alex to negotiate and I knew that would not be easy. Confrontation was inevitable and how he would take things, I couldn't predict.

"Matt! Good to see you," said Alex as he walked towards me with his hand outstretched.

"Good to see you Alex," I replied, shaking his hand.

"God, you're looking fit," he said. "Suntanned, clear eyes – your new life obviously agrees with you."

"Yes, it's good, thanks."

I got into his taxi and we headed for the restaurant where we'd had our very significant and informative lunch before. Alex had booked us there and at the same private table in the corner, obviously of the opinion that this meeting too, was to be of a private and confidential nature. We chatted on everyday matters on the journey and in the restaurant until the food was ordered, when he said to me, "What's on your mind Matt? What's imperative about it?"

"You've given Jennifer an ultimatum, Alex."

"With respect, Matt, how do you fit into that?"

That was a more subtle way of saying 'What's it got to do with you?'

"It has to do with my new life Alex. It's a fairly close knit community there, particularly around the taverna, which is a focal point. Obviously Jennifer and I have met and become friends and the goat herder, so called, is also a friend. They are naturally entitled to ask for my help if they have a problem and I naturally feel an affinity towards them as friends."

"So you're on their side!"

"If you're using blackmail of past demeanours to wreck their current wellbeing, yes, I must be on their side. I find that abhorrent!"

"Do I have to remind you that it was I who found you this wonderful location to enable your new life? And it was I who put you in the close proximity of Jennifer."

"Absolutely right Alex! But are you saying that in such circumstances I have a continual obligation to you even to the point of acquiescing to behaviour of a despicable nature?"

"So judgemental Matt and particularly without knowledge of the full facts."

"If you are referring to the terms of your marriage, you are quite right. I don't know the full facts, I don't need to know and I don't want to know. This starts and ends with blackmail and the consequent possibility of ruining people's lives. How that may or may not affect the terms of your marriage is no concern of mine.

118

So no, in that respect maybe I don't know the full facts, as you call them but it's the principal that I find abhorrent, not the facts."

"I've made it clear. If she ceases this relationship, the matter ends."

"But does it? You've seen fit to engage a private detective to gather information and compile a report, which is, by its nature on paper and there for future use. Are you simply seeking an end to a possible relationship or are you seeking some form of retribution? And in saying the matter ends, you are confirming your willingness to proceed with the blackmail if it doesn't."

He was looking a little agitated – he didn't really want a discussion about it. He clearly wanted to have his way without question. "Look, I can understand that Jennifer wants her end off occasionally, but a fucking goat herder! A FUCKING GOAT HERDER! A PRIMITIVE!" he said, then looked around anxiously, thinking he may have spoken too loudly and been overheard.

That hit me dramatically and for a number of reasons. Was he objecting because of the goat herder's assumed pedigree? Was he suggesting that had the subject of Jennifer's liaison been of a different persuasion, he would find it less objectionable, possibly even acceptable? It wouldn't have been a problem for him if I had formed the liaison as he had anticipated. Also I was surprised by his terminology of 'having her end off.' It seemed crude and out of character, both for Alex himself and for the type of woman Jennifer is.

"What is it that pains you Alex? Her having a relationship, or who she's having it with?"

"I say again Matt, a fucking goat herder! She's worth more than that!"

"So you're amenable to her having an affair, provided it's someone of your choosing or at least of your approval. Maybe your prowess in headhunting is limited to the corporate world and that emotions are best left to find their own course. Maybe Jennifer is satisfying a need that you were unaware of and can't comprehend."

"You know this man well?"

"Well enough to call him a friend. He's a very unusual man and not what you might all too readily assume. I gather he's had

119

a tough time in the past but he's got it together and made a new life. I don't want to see this new life and his contentment unravel."

"So if I stand firm, Matt, what can you or your friends do about it?"

"I was hoping you wouldn't put it that way. Have you no understanding? Have you no respect for the lives people have made for themselves whatever their past?"

"In a word no, if what they are doing is alien to me and its principles are beyond social decency."

He obviously saw it as a class violation. "Very often, the unusual can be beautiful both in its emotions and art form. It can be a powerful outlet and surely not worthy of blackmail, which, Alex, is also beyond social decency."

"I don't want to be lectured on morals, Matt."

"How would you feel if the boot was on the other foot?"

"How do you mean?"

"If maybe you had a past that you wanted forgotten." Would you still be so keen to out others?"

"Are you suggesting I have something to hide?"

"Are you confirming that you don't?"

"Don't play me with words, Matt. That may be your forte but there comes a point where substance must be added," he said, boring into me, clearly suggesting put up or shut up.

"A fourteen year old boy, wasn't it?"

I've never seen the blood drain from someone's face so quickly. He turned ashen in an instant – a living corpse. He epitomised disbelief. His fist was clenched with a slight tremor just over the table before being brought down with a thud. He was reacting involuntarily to his inner turmoil.

"How do you know about that?"

"Does that matter?"

"That is very much in the past and is not what it might seem."

"My understanding is that it is very much as it might seem."

"No charges were brought. It was dropped and it's over."

"Did the payment of his private education have a bearing on it being dropped, as you say?"

"Damn you Matt! DAMN YOU! How did you find this out? Does anyone else know?"

"I have a source and no, no-one else knows and no-one else will know, if we have an understanding."

"So you're blackmailing *me* now?"

"I wouldn't look at it quite like that but sometimes fire can only be fought with fire!"

"Anything I've done is long in the past – my past is history."

"So is his Alex. So is his!"

"What do you expect me to do?"

"Nothing! Do nothing and you will all continue to live in peace. Simply confirm to Jennifer that you will not be making any revelations, whatever her lifestyle. She doesn't deserve to be outed on a relationship."

"Look, it's vital this doesn't get out. I... I can't possibly have this coming out! How *did* you find out? This is going to haunt me now, isn't it?"

"My source is a highly skilled researcher – one of the very best! I don't know of her methods but I do know that she is very principled. She would not disclose anything unless asked to do so. I assure you it would not go beyond the three of us. If we come to an understanding, it will be closed down with no traces left. Jennifer doesn't know and neither does the goat herder and they won't. I would just tell them that we have come to an understanding."

"It sounds to me as though this source of yours could be operating illegally. The police would be interested in her."

"I don't think she had to on this occasion and the police already know of her. They use her frequently."

His face had changed now. He showed resignation. He was trembling slightly, his sole concern now that his privacy be assured. "Look, Matt. If I back off can I be assured that this won't come out?"

"Send a text to Jennifer, confirming categorically that you won't be making any disclosures that could affect their lives, and honour it, and you can be assured that my source *will* close this down and with no loose ends."

"Yes, yes, I'll do it right now," he confirmed, wanting to shake hands. As we shook, he asked, "Where does this leave us, Matt? Still friends?"

"Yes, I would hope so," I replied.

We finished our meal chatting more generally, the current matter being resolved by the text he showed me, having sent it to Jennifer there and then. It conveyed a comprehensive undertaking on his part, born out of fear of disclosure.

"Thanks for talking to me about it Matt, rather than just acting on your findings," he said as we were parting. "We've done a deal."

"Yes, we've done a deal. One thing I would say to you Alex, is that my source did say that it wasn't too difficult to get the information and it's there to be found if someone knows what they are doing and where to look."

Alex looked uneasy again. "Look," he said, "If I pay an agreed fee, would your source be able to extricate whatever led her to it or block future access in some way?"

"I don't know whether that's possible but even if it is I don't think she would do that. That I'm sure would be illegal and you're benefitting yourself from those very same principles in the way she operates."

He thought for a moment or two and then nodded. "Mm. Thanks Matt."

"I don't think you need worry too much but just be aware before you engage in any activity that may encourage that direction of enquiry."

My mission was accomplished, I would enjoy a take-away meal in my apartment, which was convenient for my stay and looked forward very much to seeing Elena tomorrow. My contentment, however, was to be short lived. I received a text from Jennifer:

Hi Matt. I have received a text from Alex confirming that he will not be making any revelations and I'm sure that's following your meeting with him for which I'm very grateful. Thank you from the bottom of my heart. It has coincided however with a visit from the police. They say Stefan has assaulted the detective and charges are possible. I don't know what to do. Jennifer.

I replied:

Thank you for telling me. I'll be back day after tomorrow and be on the case. In the meantime don't worry!
Matt.

Chapter 17

I was to meet Elena at her hotel which was arranged for the crew by her airline, close to Heathrow. She had only a short time free, having to comply with her turnaround regulations, including rest, but I had reserved a table at a restaurant not too far away for an early dinner. I had given her the choice of cuisines and she was delighted to opt for the Italian restaurant which had been a favourite of mine.

The expectation of seeing Elena was always of great joy but to meet her in London and dine with her there was completely out of context and I was ecstatic at the thought. Waiting in the hotel reception area I heard high heels on the tiled floor approaching from behind me and I knew from the particular sound that it was Elena. As I turned, I saw this familiar but intriguing woman coming towards me. Her black hair was loose over her shoulders, she was beautifully made up with her dark brown eyes accentuated and a beaming smile across her face. We embraced and as we parted, we continued to look into each other, smiling.

"You look amazing," I told her.

"So do you," said she.

The sound of high heels can be a wake-up call for many men and in that hotel reception area there wasn't one male head that failed to turn and I could sense them holding their gaze as she took my arm and we made for the door. She had a relatively short turnaround time and needed to get some sleep, so we wasted no time taking the taxi to the restaurant.

"Good evening Mr Rochester. How lovely to see you again," said the owner as we entered and addressing Elena with a slight bow of his head he added, "and we are honoured with the presence of a most beautiful signora."

"Thank you Mario," I said, as he pulled out a chair to seat Elena at our table and offered us the menus.

"Do you still get a buzz when you have time in a foreign location?" I asked.

"I do when I'm seeing you."

"Ah… it's wonderful to see *you!*"

"So which Elena am I today?"

"The one I'm looking at across this table and I do find you amazing. You certainly don't look compromised by being between flights."

"We give the girls guidance on packing for long haul flights and stopovers and I've personally honed it over the years. I limit the colours to black or navy and white or cream tops. That way everything co-ordinates and you can dress for any occasion with very little and even cover different climates. So… sightseeing, a country walk or dinner in London with a hotshot lawyer – I am covered and I make up to suit."

"Well it suits me very well. You look stunning. Thank you."

"You're very special Matt. I try to fit the occasion. From first class on the aircraft to first class in the evening."

I squeezed her hand on the table. "First class on the plane?"

"Yes, that's why I'm on this flight. We're making some changes to first class hospitality and I am there to see it implemented for a few flights. I love cuisine be it on the scheduled flights or when I'm on the prestigious charter flights where I am responsible for it – planning and discussing with clients. And talking of the cuisine I like this menu."

"Yes, Mario offers the best of Italian cooking over a wider range than the usual pastas and pizzas."

The head waiter came to take our order, the moment giving him the opportunity to exercise his Latin hot-blooded charm, well-honed when addressing highly attractive women. Elena showed appreciation of his demeanour but if he was hopeful of a more effusive response he was to be disappointed. She was world weary in that regard and excessive charm bordering on flirtation, was like water off a duck's back.

The menu offered a plate of mixed traditional starters for people to share which pleased Elena because it gave her the opportunity to sample the cuisine, and we ordered the Lemon Sole with vegetables for us both to follow. We shared a bottle of non-alcoholic wine – Elena wouldn't have alcohol before a flight.

"So, Matt, you said Jennifer and Stefanos were given an ultimatum – threat of exposure."

"Yes. So far as Stefanos is concerned, the private detective had discovered the part of his life that is now long behind him. Jennifer's husband has threatened not only to expose that, but to make her relationship with a so-called 'goat herder with a past,' known throughout her media and television circles, if she doesn't end it."

"Blackmail!"

"In a word, yes."

Elena's face contorted. "Oh the bastard! Spoil their lives!"

"In a nutshell."

"Have you managed to help, Matt? Did you meet with the husband?"

"Yes and I'd say that aspect is sorted. He's confirmed that he won't be exposing anyone now."

"How on earth did you achieve that?"

"We came to an understanding."

Elena looked puzzled. "An understanding?"

"There are many proverbs throughout history, starting with the ancient Chinese, which in effect caution against exposing other people's dirty linen if you don't have a clean sheet yourself."

"Oh, I like that!" said an amused Elena. "I love your words, as always!" She looked thoughtful for a moment or two and then said, "People in glass houses shouldn't throw stones."

"Something like that. I can't be specific – I can't disclose."

"So you played him at his own game."

"Yes but with reluctance. It is an example of doing something that is against ones principles to ameliorate a situation that is against ones principles. Fire with fire! I have used that argument in court – don't condemn them on the basis of what they have done, judge them on the outcome."

I got a tight lipped smile from her, and then she said, "You're brilliant! You do know that don't you?"

"We'll see. Whilst I have that particular aspect sorted, it seems another has come about."

"Why Matt?"

"I've had a text from Jennifer thanking me for sorting the blackmail aspect but telling me that simultaneously another situation has come about. Apparently the private detective is

125

claiming that Stefanos has assaulted him. The police are considering charges."

"Oh no! No! That can't be. Stefanos wouldn't assault anybody – unless it's self-defence."

"I agree but I don't know the circumstances."

"Poor Stefanos doesn't deserve any of this."

"I'll see what I can do when I return."

"So your information about Jennifer's husband was from your source?"

"Yes." I explained to Elena the circumstances in which I knew Jennifer's husband. "Let's just say that in the circumstances I thought it prudent to do a background check before I got involved. I like to be forearmed and with my source, it's not too difficult."

"Your source is also a private detective, presumably?"

"Not exactly. More a researcher."

"A researcher?"

"Mm… A computer genius, basically."

Elena was intrigued. "How did you meet him?"

"Her, actually. We go back a long way – I met her in my late teens. We surfed together in North Cornwall."

"And you've stayed in touch."

"Yes. We were very close then. Not romantically or even sexually linked but we found something between us that was profound at that age. She was different, very unusual and still is."

We paused while the assortment of starters was put before us. Elena was dissecting them with her eyes even before the waiter had left us and as she took some on her fork she said, "Tell me Matt. Tell me about her."

"It's a long story really and perhaps not the best dinner conversation. I'll tell you another time."

"Tell me now Matt. All conversations with you are worthy of a good dinner and I suspect this one is no different. In telling me about her, you will tell me more about you and when better than over dinner."

Elena, while enjoying sampling the starters looked at me with eager eyes. She clearly wanted me to tell her the story.

"I found this little remote cove, off the beaten track. It was small and generally devoid of tourists and the topography made it good for surfing when the winds and tides were right. It was basically just a fold in the cliffs and as the waves were funnelled in, it was a challenge, suitable only for the competent and most intrepid of surfers. It also made for quite extreme wild swimming but peaceful with just me, the seabirds, the occasional seal and the elements.

"On occasions there was another surfer there, not a body toned stereotype that you might expect in such a challenging location but a girl, and although she looked good in her wetsuit, she was quite petite and didn't immediately inspire confidence. I initially thought that she might be better suited to a location that was less demanding and had the presence of lifeguards. But she could surf. Diminutive she may have been but she was fearless, confident and had the style and balance of a ballerina. The way she moved on that board was exquisite. She would disappear from view in the trough of the waves and then re-appear on the crest swivelling to change direction and as the wave lost its momentum she came ashore as if she was bolted to the board – arms by her side and not a waver until she stepped off. I was impressed.

"She always erected a small tent at the back of the little beach for shelter. It made her seem almost a resident and I sometimes felt like an intruder. She kept herself to herself, appearing withdrawn. Even though there was usually just the two of us in that tiny cove, it took several encounters before we had more than a passing acknowledgement. Then one day the weather closed in, and as it started to rain heavily, she beckoned me over.

"I joined her in the tent and saw that she had a laptop and a chess board. There was obviously no Wi-Fi in the cove, there wasn't even a phone signal but she could use the software that was pre-loaded. She had her own world in this isolated cove. I started chatting to her but it was difficult. I thought she was socially impaired – a personality disorder maybe. But when I asked her about her computer and the chessboard, she came to life. Not animated but in a very focused way. I was astounded. Her knowledge, her concentration, the depth, the detail and the reasoning. I began to understand and was able to apply that understanding to talk with her on other subjects. She was on a different wavelength. She didn't see the world as most people see it and responded differently to almost every situation.

"She told me she had been diagnosed with Asperger's. Completely so – top end of the spectrum. She certainly exhibited many of the traits that I associate with it – social withdrawal, intensity of focus on given subjects, an aversion to noise and any form of disharmony but above all she had very high intelligence. She told me that the tests conducted on her showed her IQ to be at genius level – virtually off the scale. She told me she felt she didn't really belong in this world and she became tearful. She was shunned by her contemporaries having no interest in their conversations, social media, their topics or their everyday trivialities. She had no accord with her teachers, they saw her as having a condition and treated her accordingly but she was far more intelligent than any of them. She was desperately lonely.

"That isolated cove, was her escape. It was her refuge. It was her world where, with the absence of meaningful human contact, she could interact with the elements at an extreme level. She was there whatever the weather, embracing the loneliness and her surfing was a great skill which enabled her to connect with that world – her own world away from the mundane and I felt privileged to share part of it with her. And as we talked more, I understood and was able to see the world through her eyes and I could empathise with her.

"We'd go out together and find a wave. After a big one we'd chat about its technicalities. We'd have our packed lunch together in her tent. She'd found a friend. We had chats, long chats, very different but they suited me – often profound! I'd say she had the edge on me for chess, I had the edge on her for surfing but the conversation was probably fifty-fifty.

"I told her I thought she was quite amazing. She lit up and smiled at me. I don't think anyone had ever told her that before. She was undergoing treatment, so-called. But although they've given the condition a name, they don't know what causes it and have no cures as such. She'd had psychiatrists, psychologists and various councillors giving her therapy, trying to enable her to fit into society as we know it and she was also treated for depression. But the fact is that she is more intelligent than any of them and probably very considerably so. I told her it seemed to me that they were trying to dumb her down to their level. If they understood, they might try dumbing up everybody else, including themselves, to her level. That was the second time I saw the hint of a smile on her face and she looked into me and said 'Go on!' But that was it! Perhaps they should be learning from her, not trying to treat her."

"Did you not find a sexual attraction at that age?"

"No. I never saw her that way. Sex for its own sake would have cheapened it. It was beyond that but we effectively screwed each other's minds," I said with a chuckle. "I told her that as I saw it, she wasn't wired wrongly or with broken wires, or with a bolt missing. She didn't have a syndrome defined by being withdrawn, antisocial and excessively pedantic and all with high intelligence. It was the other way round. Her exceptional intelligence barred her from normal social interaction which caused her to be withdrawn, appearing antisocial and unduly focused because she couldn't identify with what everyone else was talking about or interested in, the everyday humdrum and the pettiness. She wanted more and it wasn't there. These were the effects of her IQ which itself was the prime factor. She could have been from a different planet. In convincing her that she had a named condition they had just compounded her self-doubt and her loneliness.

"Believe in yourself and be the free spirit that you are and always look for the biggest wave in whatever you are doing, I told her."

Our main course was put before us and it looked delicious. Baked Lemon Sole in a sauce, with aubergines, potatoes and some fresh herbs. Elena's eyes were all over it and her nostrils feasted on the aromas. "Wow," she said, thanking me profusely for what we were about to receive.

As she delicately set about dissecting the fish, she was eager to continue the conversation. "What's her name, Matt?"

"Cathy."

"Yes for some reason she sounds like a Cathy. You helped her Matt. You helped her a lot."

"In helping her to accept the world differently, I helped myself. I realised that I too could move through life retaining the free spirit that I was when I met her. Surfing and the freedom that went with it and it's connections to reality didn't have to be a stage that I moved through before a more sedate or mundane academic life replaced it, only to be replaced again by the next stage as I progressed towards senescence. I too then saw the world differently gaining a greater belief in *myself* and always sought the biggest wave in whatever *I* was doing at any given time. One of my tutors at Oxford told me that at some stage I must decide whether I saw my life on a surfboard or in a courtroom. I told him 'both.' He didn't realise it at the time but he had unwittingly nailed it! In always seeking the biggest wave I would be continually surfing and if I can't find that elusive wave, I would do the same as I would in the ocean – move elsewhere to find it.

"But her biggest break was to come after she'd gone to university. I had a meeting with one of the foremost computer researchers in the business. I had a case where I needed briefing in that subject at that level. Whilst lunching with him I told him about Cathy and about her extraordinary ability with computers. More than a penchant, it was a calling. He looked into me fiercely and after a few moments said that he would like to meet her. He told me that more than fifty percent of his employees have Asperger's – so-called. He also said that he understood that a large proportion of the major breakthroughs at NASA had come from people with Asperger's. 'But don't worry about it, they're working on a cure,' he added sarcastically. He too was of the opinion that in many cases the traits were simply due to the high intelligence.

"I put them in touch and he drove all the way down to North Devon from London to meet her. He stayed at an inn there and met with her over two days. He offered her a job on the spot, with a salary that would ensure she was not tempted elsewhere and provided an apartment in London for her. I don't think her feet have touched the ground since. She's worked on classified government work as well as for the private sector and is in her element. She's worked with people who in the main speak the same language and think the same way. They bounce off each other.

"She now has contentment. She can live her life with confidence of who she is but it's more than a psychological transformation. On a practical level, her brain is functioning at the level it is capable of. It's like the smoothness of a powerful engine humming at or above the cruising speed for which it was designed."

"Has she changed a lot?"

"She's still basically the Cathy that I first met and got to know well but she has matured somewhat. Above all she is very confident and presents very much as her own person. The last time I saw her, she had dark purple hair and her right arm was completely covered in tattoos but she was well groomed."

"Does she still surf?"

"Very much so but now she drives down in her Porsche with her boards on a roof rack. If I say she is unusual, believe it! She works for herself now. They helped to set her up on the basis that she still does a lot of work for them. She's ok and I'm so pleased for her.

"So no... no relationship as such but an affinity was gained at what was a very formative part of our lives. She as a person, our philosophical discussions... it was very meaningful for both of us. It altered her world and it certainly enabled me to re-assess myself, to better understand who I was and to enable me to express myself – my inner spirit as I progressed. I would not become a stereotype. We are very different people and have followed diverse paths but there will always be a bond. You're the first person I've told about her, apart from the guy who took her on."

"Thanks Matt," she said touching my arm. "Thank you for telling me. I'd like to meet her if the opportunity presents. She sounds amazing and so are you. I've learnt a lot more about you too."

"How's the meal?"

"Exquisite! These aubergines are incredible. It's the marinade. I'd love to know what it is."

"Mm... I don't think he'd be about to tell you."

"Then we must prise it out of him," said Elena with a subtle smile crossing a determined face. "I think we have need of your words, Matt."

"Didn't you tell me that you did a course on hypnosis?"

"Yes, while I was at university."

"Right! I think you may stand a better chance with that than with my words. The waiter is already entranced by your presence, it wouldn't take much hypnosis to captivate him fully."

"And with the right words from you, Matt, they would be giving us their secrets without realising they were doing it. It would be like a sting!"

"I think Mario's recipes would be family secrets passed down but not easily passed on. They would be locked away in his safe."

"So you see it more as a safe breaking operation."

"A bit drastic for an aubergine marinade recipe, don't you think?"

"Oh no! We'd go for the fish sauce recipe as well. That too is pretty amazing!"

"Mm… I think that must be for another day," I told a highly amusing Elena.

"Maybe but we can case the place while we're here. Note the locks, positions of cameras."

I had to laugh. "Are they really that good?" I asked.

"They are superb!"

And at that moment we were approached my Mario. "Was everything to your liking?" he asked as the waiter removed our plates from the table.

"It was excellent," said an enthused Elena. The aubergine's marinade was exquisite," she added using her fingers in emphasis.

Mario leaned to her and in a semi whisper as if telling her a secret, said, "Orange peel." The look on Elena's face was also exquisite as he left us.

"Not even hypnosis was necessary," I told her.

"Orange peel my foot! Orange oil is very pungent. If it was in that marinade I would have picked up on it." I had to laugh. I found it all so amusing. "What do you find so funny Matt Rochester?"

"Don't you see? It's you that's been stung."

"Oh yes I see alright! I won't even bother to pick the locks. I'll just break a window!" She was delightful.

We laughed and laughed together, the other diners intrigued as to what was so amusing. "Oh Matt," said Elena. "I've so loved this evening. The venue, the food, the conversation, the fun.

132

Thank you so much. I've never had conversations like we have – ever! We go from the profound to the flippant – from tears, almost, to laughter and all in a world of our own."

"You're wonderful!" I told her. "I love every minute. Will you be ok for time?" I asked, looking at my watch.

"Yes. I will get my rest. No brandy and cigarette outside under the old lantern tonight but I'll be coming home tomorrow Matt," she added, touching my arm. "I may even be back before you."

Chapter 18

My return flight was later in the day and Elena was indeed back before me. As I walked towards the taverna, I saw her sitting outside with some locals and I noticed that two of them were smoking her black cigarettes.

"High Matt," said she, enthusiastically as she got up and came over to me with her usual lovely smile. She put her cheek to mine as we held each other's arms. "Lovely to see you back."

"And you. I see you're corrupting the locals," I told her.

She looked puzzled and turned to look at the locals she had been sitting with and then seeing them puffing on their cigarettes, she laughed. She turned back to me and in a softened voice said, "Our turn tonight under the old lantern. I've seen Jennifer. She's very upset about Stefanos."

"Yes, I know. I've spoken to her on the phone today. She's going to fill me in this evening in the taverna and has asked me if I will be present tomorrow at a meeting she has requested with the police here – which of course I will."

"He smokes – the policeman apparently. According to Jennifer"

"The locals, you, me, the policeman, you're not going to run out are you?"

"Look, don't ever worry about that!" I was told before she turned to re-join the locals.

Jennifer was at the bar as I walked into the taverna that evening. I gestured towards a table by the wall and she came over to join me.

"You must have a drink this time," she said.

"No honestly, I'm fine." I told her. "I will enjoy my wine with my meal"

"Then I will arrange a bottle for you with Elena. I absolutely insist."

"So, tell me exactly what has happened and how it came about," I said as we sat down.

"Apparently the private detective visited Stefan on his farm."

134

"Was he invited?"

"No."

"Had he made an appointment?"

"No, he just turned up. As he walked towards Stefan, he kicked one of his many cats out of the way. Stefan told him, as Stefan would, 'Hey man, don't hurt my cats,' but he promptly did it again. Stefan warned him again, 'I've told you man leave my cats alone – you hurt them, I hurt you!' But he was going for another one. Stefan ran to him with his finger pointing, whereupon the detective backed away, stumbled, fell backwards and hit his head on the hard ground at that point. He was dazed but when he got up he immediately accused Stefan of assault. He's told the police that he was head-butted. His head was bleeding at the side of his forehead and he went straight to the police."

"Any witnesses?"

"No. The police are considering charges and he is talking of a private case against Stefan, for damages."

"And we have this meeting tomorrow with the policeman?"

"Yes, as arranged."

"Good. I look forward to it! In the meantime don't worry and tell Stefan the same. Ok?"

"Yes. Thanks Matt and thank you again so much for getting the understanding with my husband. I don't know how you managed that but both Stefan and I are so very grateful. There must be some costs involved, both with your source as you say and of course with your time."

"No, no. I can't go into detail but my research was initiated primarily for my benefit and I was going to London anyway for meetings with clients. I simply altered the times to suit, so just regard it all as help from a friend to both of you."

"Bless you," she said, showing some emotion. I'm eating with Stefan away from here. It's shattered his peace. He needs support."

Elena and I dined together in the taverna that evening and it was amazing to think that we had just the previous night dined together in London. It was so relaxed. We talked about the restaurant and the menu. Elena had asked her mother about orange peel in the aubergine marinade and she said the same thing – that to them it would have been obvious. They have known of orange peel used in some marinades, with certain meats in particular but it is usually obvious by its pungency. She also wanted to know more about Cathy – she really was intrigued.

We sat out under the lantern and had our usual brandy and shared a cigarette. "Would you mind if I sat in on the meeting with the police tomorrow? Jennifer suggested it. I could offer him a cigarette," said she with a chuckle "but Jennifer said I should ask you, obviously. It would be quite usual for a lawyer to have his PA with him, wouldn't it? But in this case, unbeknown to him, I would be there as a muse."

"You think I might need inspiration?"

"No, I don't. I'd just like to feel part of it, knowing you as I do."

"It's fine by me but be careful about offering a policeman one of those cigarettes. You might find yourself in a situation where my words would be of no consequence."

She laughed. "Look these are branded," said she showing me the packet. "It's the ones I roll myself that might be contentious."

"You are priceless, Elena Costopolou," I told her.

The policeman arrived mid-morning as Jennifer had arranged and we three sat at a secluded table outside. Jennifer introduced Elena and myself to the officer and coffees were arranged.

"So, Mr Rochester, I understand you will represent Stefanos." I noted that he referred to him by his christian name which suggested he knew him as did most people in this area. "You understand you have to be registered to practice in Greece, in order to do that."

"If he wants me to represent him I could do so through a Greek lawyer but that would only apply if he is charged with an offence which according to the facts I've been given, would seem unlikely."

"You realise we are talking of assault here. The complainant was injured. Do you have evidence to offer?"

"Do you have evidence of a crime by Stefanos?"

"Unfortunately for him it would seem to be quite obvious."

"But I asked you if you have any evidence because without it, it becomes less obvious."

"Stefanos threatened him and then carried out the threat by head-butting the complainant, causing injury from which he fell to the ground."

"That's not evidence, that's one side of the story. Stefanos tells it differently and without independent witnesses it's simply one's word against the other."

"And that Mr Rochester is what is being considered by the police."

I leaned to him and put a little more assertion in my voice. "So let us for the purpose of this consideration start at the beginning and present a logical scenario. The complainant entered the property without prior arrangement and without permission. That could be construed as trespass. His first action was to kick one of Stefan's cats which could bring the word aggravated to the trespass. Stefanos asked him not to hurt his cats but he proceeded to do it again. Stefanos then warned him not to do it again saying 'You hurt them, I hurt you.' That is a warning not a threat and it was a warning your complainant didn't heed. He proceeded to do it a third time whereby stefanos started to run towards him holding his fingers out as a pointer of blame. The complainant was startled, probably fearful of the situation he had caused, backed away, stumbled and fell backwards, hitting his head on the hard ground. There was no head- butt. Martial artists rarely use head-butts – it's not in their remit. They are generally not part of their training and are not necessary with the repertoire they have at their disposal. That wouldn't be a consideration for Stefanos and in the circumstances certainly not necessary. Also the wound sustained by the complainant is not that of a head-butt, which would be full frontal to the face. The wound was to the side, consistent with hitting the ground as he twisted"

"He says he turned his head away at the point of impact."

"A head-butt can only be executed if they are standing face to face and would be instantaneous. He wouldn't have time turn his head away and even if he did, the wound is more likely to be bruising rather than a laceration. He's lying! Stefanos is not a violent man – just the opposite. In the absence of witnesses it must be viewed on the circumstances and it would seem that this guy came to Stefan's farm with the intention of causing trouble

– possibly even to enable a false charge. But it seems to me that we would be in a better position to press charges against him."

The officer said nothing as he looked into me in thought for some moments. Then as if coming to the present, he jerked his head somewhat and said, "Look, I know Stefanos is respected and well liked around here and from what little I know of him I would go along with that but you will understand I had to put forward the complaint."

"Which you have done and now have the complete picture."

"Would you like a cigarette?" asked Elena. Holding the packet towards him with one loose to be taken.

"They're unusual," said he. "Long and black. Turkish?"

"No, Indonesian. They're clove induced. They used to be available in Greece but I don't think they are now."

"Could... could I take one to try later," he asked.

"Of course. Please do," said Elena, amiably.

He took one appreciatively and said, "I'll have to confer on this but I can't see it being taken any further."

"Thank you for coming to see us," I said.

He then stood up immediately, thanked us for the coffee and Elena again for the cigarette as we all shook hands and he made for his car.

I turned to Elena and told her, "Your timing was brilliant! Absolutely brilliant."

She laughed. "Thank you. Oh I enjoyed that! I'd say that's another win under your belt," said Elena and then snuggling up to me and putting her arm through mine, she said in playful tones," As a hotshot lawyer's muse in disguise as an acting PA, did I make a positive contribution?"

"Extremely positive. At the point where there was nothing else to say on the matter, we were on the home straight and you subtly took us over the finish line."

"Oh I enjoyed that too," said Jennifer. "Wonderful! Thank you so much Matt," she added as she got up and embraced me. "Thank you," she said again looking into my face. "And you too Elena. Thanks for everything!" And we each high fived, signifying a job done.

"Look Jennifer, I propose phoning Alex to express my displeasure at what's happened. If you would like to be present, I could do it now."

"Yes please," was her immediate response.

I phoned him while we were at the table outside the taverna: "Hello Matt," said Alex, answering his phone.

"Hello Alex. Is it convenient to talk? Have you got a few moments?"

"Yes. What's on your mind Matt?"

"Alex, your private detective is still here and making a nuisance of himself. He's confronted the goat herder on his farm in what seems to be a deliberate attempt to cause trouble. He was kicking his adopted cats despite being warned and is claiming he was assaulted by the herder trying to get the police to bring charges. Well I don't think that is going to happen but why is he still here? Call him off Alex!"

"I've told him our arrangement is over. It ended with his report and I'm not paying him for anything further."

"Well I don't think he's got the message. Either he feels he is still under instruction or he is conducting a personal vendetta. You do realise that he is not registered to one of the bodies governing private investigators don't you? That means he is basically a law unto himself."

"I engaged the only one who could undertake the job at such short notice – virtually immediately. He seemed quite reasonable."

"Well I suggest you contact him and get him to withdraw immediately. He seems like a loose cannon and likely to cause more trouble for the people here than he already has, or for you Alex! I've already had to meet the police today to sort out what he's done and I must make it perfectly clear that we don't want any further intrusion."

"I understand Matt. I'm sorry for what he now seems to be doing. I will contact him and insist he ceases and leaves the area."

"Thank you Alex. I hope he listens."

"Thank you for phoning, Matt."

Stefanos came over to Elena and me as he entered the taverna that evening and embraced both of us. "I owe you man," he said, "for this and for stopping the blackmail. Thanks man," he reiterated.

"You owe me nothing," I told him, still in his embrace. He looked into me and I saw the inner man – a beautiful person. I told him, "Don't let it linger in your mind, Stefan. It's just a small part of this world that's passed through. Consciously be at peace. It's over!"

Chapter 19

Elena had a few days off and we spent most of that time together. It had become the norm when she was home – swimming, drives into the mountains for walks and lunch in remote tavernas. We wanted to be together. She would often read through my progressing manuscript and was very helpful with the discussions that followed but she was vexed that I hadn't yet got a title. I'd had a few ideas but they weren't right and Elena agreed – okay but not the one that was sought.

It was the last day of her leave that we were to go to the dance I had pre-booked at the venue in the mountains and we were both looking forward to it. I think we both saw it as a catalyst in our relationship. By its very nature it would be intimate and the venue evocative.

The setting was spectacular. A rugged mountain landscape with the jagged ruins of an ancient monastery partly silhouetted against the skyline. It was evocative – romantic, conjuring mystery and intrigue. It had been partially renovated – its walls cleaned up and with some apex roofing giving limited shelter here and there but it was mostly open to the skies. Extensive concrete flooring made it suitable as a venue for various events.

We arrived relatively early – the band was still setting up and the catering facilities in preparation. But quite a few people were there and most noticeably men, either individuals or in groups

"I thought most men came late, just to get a drink and see if there are any spares," I said.

Elena had a look of distain on her face. "No," she said. The earlier they come, the more drink they can get in and they don't want to miss out on any opportunities that may arise from the start. Notice they are all near and facing the entrance so they can examine the arrivals. If women arrive, they would converge like a flock of vultures but rather than to devour their prey, they would exercise their innate passion."

"You know the drill well."

"Oh, very well! As I said, I could never come here or to similar events on my own."

A waiter showed us to our table and we ordered drinks. Non-alcoholic – I was driving and Elena said she may have a glass of wine with her food. The conversation continued to flow in earnest – we hadn't stopped talking from the time we set off. There were rarely any breaks in the conversation between us and this night was certainly no exception.

She was telling me more about her job with the airline – the work she does and some unusual situations that have arisen, as one can imagine. She also talked about the taverna, her love of cooking and Greek cuisine in particular, which was a passion and she talked again about the Italian food we had in the London restaurant. She clearly enjoyed that.

Having got our drinks, she leaned closer to me over the table and asked me more about Cathy – she really was most intrigued. She certainly found her story fascinating but also I thought that she was concerned to know the extent to which we were still linked. I'd told her there never was a relationship there but to Elena she obviously remained a female link in my life.

"So you have a relationship but with non-attachment."

She was back on that one. "Look, we don't have and never have had a relationship as such, so attachment either non or otherwise doesn't apply."

"You are both lone individuals in your own way and you obviously have a bond. I can see you going off together at some time looking for that bigger wave – a remote island, surfing, writing, playing chess."

I nodded my head as if to agree with her. "You didn't mention riding on the backs of whales or the wings of giant manta rays. We would walk up the silver path to the moon and enter nirvana holding hands."

"I am serious!" said she with a smile on her face.

"So am I!" There is no relationship – there never was. I never saw her that way and I don't think she did me, if she did, she didn't show it. Our conversations were never in the slightest romantic or sexual. Deep, profound, philosophical but never romantic and in any case I think she prefers the company of women to men."

"Really?"

"Yes. I don't know for sure – we've never talked about personal matters and certainly not persuasions but when she was in her apartment in London I saw her there with another girl and although it was not made obvious, I got that impression. Now she has a converted sail loft in North Devon and on the few occasions I've been there, I have seen or known of an older lady and I get the same impression. Cathy is a similar age to me – 35ish – her companion must be late forties maybe fifties, quite attractive and well presented. She's an artist."

The waiter came and took our orders for food. Having a table, we were waited on. Others had to buy as a take away from the stalls.

"Does she live with the artist? Are they together?"

"I don't know. I don't think she lived with the girl in London but she may well spend a lot of time with the artist in Devon. I'm pleased for her. She needs a sexual outlet like everyone else but if it is more of a meaningful relationship to her, again I'm happy for her. As we've said, she's very different and to find someone who suits her cannot be easy and I can't see the male ego surviving her capabilities."

Elena found that amusing. "Yes, *I* find that difficult – *she* must find it impossible!" she laughed openly. "There are of course exceptions to the norm," she added putting her hand on mine. She continued to laugh, put her finger to my nose and pressed it.

"Well at least you've ensured a continuation of our evening," I told her. With her lips tightly closed she continued to stifle a laugh. She always loved to tease me and it was endearing.

Our chosen food from the limited menu was put before us together with a glass of white wine for Elena. We had pizzas with a side salad and the inevitable small bowl of chips. Elena looked at it and again with closed lips, she waved her head from side to side as if to say 'It could be worse.' The menu was limited by their ability to cook with the mobile facilities and a pizza from the flame oven seemed appropriate.

The conversation didn't pause for the food to be eaten and that was an art that I had honed since knowing Elena. The band was now playing and some people were dancing in the open area and we would join them once we'd finished our meal

A half-light provided by shaded lamps on the tables and the moonlight giving a silvery balm where there were no canopies created an evocative, moody atmosphere in the ruins as twilight approached.

Elena's presence was quite different to that which I had experienced to date. She clearly liked dancing, being expressive but with reserved competency. She could dance but she was not flamboyant – there was a reservation about her that gave her dignity and grace. But by its very nature dancing was intimate – the music, the contact and the movement. I had walked with her, swum with her and in remote situations, I'd dined with her and had intimate conversations but this was very different. The atmosphere between us seemed charged and it was really lovely. I felt so privileged to be in such a situation with someone like Elena and judging by the eyes of men that were focussing on her, any thoughts that I had were not exclusive to me.

She was wearing what I know as a tunic dress in a fine fabric in a very deep red, contrasting with her black hair but overall it gave a subdued, subtle, arty effect. Sophisticated bohemian almost. The dress was a close fit but not figure hugging, it hung beautifully with her figure around her loins being emphasised only as she moved.

By her movement and her subtle looks, she appeared to be flirting with me. She picked up on my looks and gave me some wonderful smiles. She came to me, we held each other and danced in unison as the music slowed and wow! If the atmosphere between us had been amplifying since we first met, it was now fully charged. I could feel her hair brushing against my face, I could smell that subtle unusual perfume of hers, which she told me was vintage Greek and in our dance hold, I could feel her body movement on her heels which was bordering on the erotic. My manhood was stirring and I was conscious that it might be detected as we came into closer contact but if one of the occasional smiles she was giving me was in acknowledgement of that, I wasn't to know.

As the evening progressed, most people were dancing in some form or another and occasionally, the band played the typical music for traditional Greek dancing. The pronounced beat and the sound of balalaikas emphasised. Elena took great delight in giving me instruction as we lined up, hands on the next persons shoulders as we moved rhythmically sideways, one way and then the other. As the music got faster and faster, she demonstrated her prowess as she joined others in the centre. She was very good, clearly enjoying herself and was visually quite striking.

When the dance finished and individuals returned to their partners, Elena was approached by a man as she was making her way back to me. She slowed but didn't stop as they chatted briefly. She resumed her walk to me but he caught her up and spoke again. She turned on him and whilst I couldn't hear what was said, cordiality soon ended as Elena became visibly assertive.. I walked towards her in case she needed my presence but she sorted it and met me with a smile, seemingly unperturbed. She came close and put her arm around me and I her, pulling her tightly to me.

"Are you okay?" I asked.

"I'm fine," she replied.

"Was he untoward?"

"His first approach was polite. He asked me if I would dance with him. I was equally polite in telling him I am with someone. His second approach was crude, so he got the answer he deserved." She turned her face to mine and said with a lovely smile. "It's fine Matt, nothing too much out of the ordinary."

We danced and we danced, some rock music, some smooching and all under a starry sky with the light of the moon. It felt wonderful to me and Elena was clearly in her element. We were very close. At midnight, the band finished with more Greek dancing numbers and it was time to leave. I didn't want it to end – the music, the atmosphere but above all, the sheer bliss of the closeness and shared intimacy with Elena.

We walked to the car and once inside we just looked at each other face to face for a while, our eyes locked, silently in the moon's silvery darkness. I lightly traced the features of her face with my finger and round to her ear. I spread my fingers through her hair, combing it slowly several times from her temple to below her shoulders and we rubbed noses. The atmosphere between us was charged and our heads were drawn to one instinctively and we kissed. Our lips were entwined, each softly exploiting the other for greater sensation. I was off the ground, floating, mesmerised. Elena had a presence – a great presence, always there when we were together. It projected, it was almost palpable and particularly when we were walking side by side. But now, kissing her, it was being transmitted live through our lips. It was like an electric current and I was heady, transfixed – otherworldly.

History tells us that in ancient times, the fate of nations has fallen to such allure and if any were to doubt that feasibility, then they should have been in my shoes at that moment. I was utterly captivated – beyond reason. And I wanted more. All that I had felt during my time with her was coming together in one moment and my headiness was overwhelming. I was aware of so much but couldn't define anything. That subtle perfume was as an incense from ancient ethers, I heard words that weren't spoken, I had sensations unknown to me before that moment and my feelings sought the words to express them. She sensed I was about to speak and put her finger to my lips. She stiffened somewhat and moving away slightly, with calm authority said, "Matt, I'm not on the pill!"

Our intimacy was severed instantly. Her statement required an answer and I didn't immediately have one. What could I say? It doesn't matter – but it does! Don't worry about that – but in essence we should! We can still be close without full sex – the ultimate platitude! The right answer was difficult to find without consideration and it was that pause that was the return to reason and sanity that killed the moment. It wasn't so much that the answer wasn't forthcoming, it was more that her statement was the wrong one at the wrong time.

That she was not on the pill did of course matter, as things were progressing but progression would have been in her room or mine and that would surely be the right time for her to inform me. But not as a cold statement – surely as whispered words as part of our progression. As it was it was a definite break, a bucket of cold water and as I knew Elena, it wasn't an unfortunate remark or simply with bad timing, it was deliberate. Not designed to hurt or as a put down but it was more than a cautionary consideration, it was an involuntary closure of our intimacy. On that chapter, the last of the evening's beautiful story, the curtain fell. I knew that but I didn't know why.

I drove us back to the taverna bemused. What had I said? What had I done? We had been so close ever since our first encounter and my surprise was that its natural progression hadn't culminated before now – God knows we had the moments, the opportunities. Perhaps that's the answer. That there is some reason why we haven't shared the ultimate intimacy and the occasion tonight brought that reason into play.

And I felt almost angry. I felt let down. I didn't want to show presumption or coerce her in any way. Above all it had to be two way. In not kissing her before or making any physical moves upon her, I was respecting her will and her integrity. It was strange. We were so close and to all intents intimate but we hadn't come on to each other. Tonight was the catalyst. I was surely entitled to foresee the ultimate intimacy and heaven knows I needed that outlet – it's been so long. So long with a man's imagination conjuring what hasn't been available and almost to the point of overload at times and then the closeness with Elena has taken that need almost to breaking point. I cannot take a woman purely for sexual outlet either by mutual consent or by paying for it and the onset of the most natural of progressions and with someone like Elena would be the ultimate release. But for some reason it wasn't to be and yes I felt angry. But that anger wasn't directed at Elena, it was more of an inner turmoil by virtue of it happening.

"What's wrong?" I asked her in an endearing way as we pulled into the taverna car park. But I got no answer. She simply looked into me in the darkness and she held her look, eventually leaning to me and whispering.

"Thank you for tonight. It was wonderful." And then she kissed my forehead and said, before getting out of the car, "I'll text you!"

She was leaving for duty in the morning.

Chapter 20

I felt a great loneliness.

I always felt a loss when Elena went away but it was tempered with the knowledge that we were virtually "together" as a couple and that she would return soon. But this time it was very different. The closeness had been taken away in an instant. There was a problem and I didn't know what it was. I expected the text from her that she said she would send but it didn't come. I had hoped that it might contain an explanation that she hadn't felt able to give in person. Three days passed and I heard nothing from her. I had tried to compile a text for her but that didn't feel right. I had asked her to her face what was wrong and in the absence of her promised text it felt wrong.

In my room that evening I broke down. I couldn't help it. I loved her. I truly loved her like never before and it had gone and I didn't know why. I went through our time together, reliving the moments, searching for possible clues but they weren't to be found. Maybe it was her personality – that she had an ingredient that wouldn't allow her to become too close and when the moment came, it surfaced. That had to be it and if so, there was nothing I could do about it.

Stefan wanted us to go surfing but the winds were too light to offer the possibility of decent waves. As he rightly said, "We won't waste our time. It would be more like paddle boarding." He reckoned there wasn't even enough for kite surfing and that too was a disappointment because I was eager to give that a go. He was apologetic, "I'm sorry man," he said, as if it was his fault that we had to cancel our plans.

"Hey, don't apologise," I told him. "It's not your fault. I will look forward to when the wind is up."

In the absence of surfing, he invited me to his little farm to see his humble abode and have lunch with him. Knowing of this, Jennifer said why not take the occasion to combine it with a visit to her villa, which she had previously suggested, which I gladly accepted. It would all surely help to take my mind off things.

I was in good time, so not wanting to arrive early, when not too far away, I pulled off the road and walked a short way to a vantage point to see the landscape. I saw Stefan's farm ahead, just off the road as it snaked its way through the mountains – instantly recognisable by the Harley Davidson parked alongside the small dwelling. The single storey oblong stone building looked isolated with no other buildings in its immediate proximity, apart from what looked like a small barn.

And as I looked from a distance, from that higher ground, I saw his world in one snapshot. I saw the farm, primitive and lonely in its mountain setting, I saw his motorcycle and his rusty iconic van at rest, I saw his cats, some wandering some lazing and I saw goats in the vicinity. But above all, I saw Stefan and he was working out and to me that was a privilege. It was more than a workout – it was a spiritual alignment. He was at one with all that surrounded him both physically and ethereally. He was going through a routine but not as I had seen him before, briefly with his Qigong ritual, this was unmistakably Kung Fu. And whilst his Qigong was remarkable for its beauty of execution, his Kung Fu was astounding. I had seen martial artists working out before but never like this. His movements were at times warrior-like but his intentions were not to an aggressor, they were as a discipline between his being and a greater force. He was becoming at one with everything that there is and in achieving this his physicality seemed to alter. The outlines of his body seemed hazy as if he was between one state of being and another. His movements flowed with effortless strength, where like a ballet dancer, physical difficulty had been overcome with endless practice in the execution of beauty and art. This was a man whose whole being and understanding had been transformed by a dedicated two years in a remote monastery. Yes, I had a snapshot of his life and its meaning.

But as I later drove onto his farm, that snapshot became my reality. On leaving my car I was at once amid a flurry of cats, each vying for attention. Stefan appeared and coming over to me, he said, "Welcome to my humble abode, man."

"It feels lovely, "I told him. "And this setting," I added, gesturing about me, "It's magical!"

149

And it was – surreal almost in its simplicity. He led me inside, accompanied by several of the cats, giving the impression that they too were welcoming me to their home and wow, it was like stepping back in time. Single story, one area without partition and high ceilinged with exposed rounded timbers. There was a log burner for heating on chilly nights, a stone bread oven in a cooking area and his bed was at one end as a sleeping area. The atmosphere was heady with incense, which could be seen smoking from little bowls here and there and the stone floor had a scattering of rugs which the cats put to good use. It was comical almost, with several of them stretched out on their backs adding to the laid back environment that surrounded Stefan.

He took me to the cooking area and showing me his bowl of home-made soup on the cooker, he gave me a spoonful to sample. "Okay for you?" he asked.

"Very good," I told him. And it was. Green lentils, onion and broken pieces of Feta cheese sprinkled on top, with olive oil and red wine vinegar to add to taste and his home-made wholemeal crusty bread. It was simplicity itself, probably much as it would be in a monastery, wholesome, totally unpretentious and utterly delicious.

"Love this Stefan." I told him.

"Thanks man," he said. "The whole process – sourcing, preparing, cooking and eating nourishes both the body and the soul."

"As does everything in your life now, Stefan and it's a pleasure to share some of it with you."

"Thanks man. You're welcome anytime, really!"

We chatted at length and showing me around, he introduced me to some of his goats, who were also friendly, if not curious. He has quite a number but they function mainly as pets, being kept purely for their milk. One of the larger nearby farms processes the milk for cheese which is his main outlet and the neighbouring farms help him out when necessary as he does them.

I went on to Jennifer's villa which was not too far away, set on high ground just off the road on the edge of the mountains.

It was traditional and renovated to preserve its originality. The only obvious nod to modernity was the small swimming pool just beyond the terrace. It was truly a renovation rather than a conversion and it was expertly done. I could see the skill of Stefan in the woodwork, some renovated, some replaced but all in keeping with the original. Where new wood was used, it was subtly aged. With stone or tiled floors, roughly rendered walls and exposed rounded timbers on the ceilings the atmosphere was amazing. There was still some finishing work to be done but Jennifer was hopeful of moving in shortly.

We sat out on the terrace under a high reed awning with tea and some little Greek specialities. "Did you make these?" I asked.

"No, I don't have the facilities here yet. They are with the compliments of Elena. She loves playing around in the kitchen when she has some spare time, which is not a lot since you've been here," she added with a smile. "When is she due back?"

"I... I don't know to be honest. I think she's on extended duty."

"I like Elena," said Jennifer. "I like her a lot. Stunningly attractive, intelligent and mature for her years. She's a class act and I've got a lot of time for her. The airline think the world of her – she's got executive status there as I'm sure you know. She is literally a high flier but with her feet firmly on the ground. For all her high profile life in that world, including some of the private jets, she is still of this place. She is frequently to be seen sitting, chatting and laughing with the locals sharing her... unusual cigarettes. She is a lovely and very special person. They all love her, men and women, young and old – to a man wouldn't you say?" said Jennifer giving me an old fashioned look. "And with all the opportunities she must have had and all the attention she still gets, it's *you* that she's in love with!"

Jennifer's appraisal of Elena and her sentiments played havoc with my emotions which had been tenuously held together for the last few days and it robbed me of the words for an immediate answer. There was a protracted silence between us and I could feel moisture in my eyes which must have been apparent to Jennifer.

"When *is* she coming back Matt?" she asked again, in a tone suggestive of a friendly inquisition.

I shook my head. "I don't know," I had to answer and the confession brought my emotions to a head. I'd kept them pretty much in check since that first night, certainly while I'm in public but Jennifer had exposed the weakness. I had to keep my lips clenched tightly to suppress them.

"Oh God! What's happened between you two Matt?"

"I don't know. We got close at the dance and she backed off. Too close, obviously. I don't know what's wrong."

Jennifer looked at me intensely for a moment then she leaned to me across the table and said, "You do know how much she's in love with you, don't you?"

"That's intuition is it?"

"It's more than that but I'll throw it in as well."

"You've spoken to her?"

"She has spoken to me. I wouldn't disclose our conversation but I'll tell you this. She fell in love with you the first time you spoke to her and it's just grown and grown. It's bloody obvious Matt! I can see it in her eyes. She lights up when you're around and when you are not, whether she is behind the bar or sitting with the locals, her eyes are secretly hoping for you to appear. She has a facility in Athens and an apartment in Thessaloniki provided by the airline to stay-over between spells of duty but I don't think she's used them since you've been here. I've never seen her around so much. Even when she's with others, her eyes are looking out for you and when you're together, the air between you crackles. She's never felt like this before and she's frightened. I know she is!"

"Frightened?"

"Yes, frightened. Frightened to cross a certain line fearing that you are just passing through – that sooner or later you will move on. She's deeply passioned Matt, her feelings are from deep within. She's in turmoil now – crossing that line could break her, strong as she is, unless she knows she's safe."

My emotions were obvious now. "I'm not going anywhere," I managed to get out.

"She doesn't know that."

"And now she's gone. Oh God, Jennifer! I haven't read it properly. I should have talked to her. Yes we've been very close as must be obvious but I haven't come on to her directly, feeling it would be an intrusion, not having long been here and she is very much her own person. Likewise, she hasn't come on to me and I've thought that is possibly for similar reasons." I put my hands to my head. "Yes, I'm in love with her – utterly!"

"Yes, that's obvious too Matt. They say that in this world, our soulmates are constantly searching for each other. You two were made for each other so it's got to be sorted and if nature can't handle it in the true course of events, I'll give it a helping hand."

"Like?"

"Like banging your heads together for a start." She leaned across the table, put her hand on my shoulder and said, "Contact her Matt. Contact her!"

She walked with me to the door and once more told me with a look of serious intent in her eyes "You must contact her."

I turned and embraced her as we said goodbye and nodded, saying to her, "Thanks Jennifer. Thanks for talking to me!"

I was now seeing it differently and it began to make sense. But even if Jennifer was right, there was no need to handle it the way she did and I didn't think I deserved the upset that I've had. But I too might have read the situation and spoken to her earlier but pointing out misunderstandings wasn't called for here. Yes, I *would* contact her. I'd send her a text but how would I word it? I thought it over and over and whilst eating my meal in the taverna that evening I did a few drafts in my writing folder but none of them felt right. How do I reach her? And then I thought, just tell her naturally how I feel and what it means to me and if Jennifer's assessment of things is about right, it should give her the opportunity to respond. I sent this text.

I walk along the beach to the lonely coves but the solitude is now unbearable. I have lunch in a mountain taverna but the chair opposite me is empty. The music in your taverna no longer reaches my heart and my room is no longer a place of sanctuary but of loneliness. Nothing is the same. I'm so lonely because you see, I love you so very much and I miss you! 'My heart is sore pained within me.' Where are you?

If you wish to receive further texts like this: *reply with a kiss.*

If you wish to unsubscribe: *I'm sorry but this link does not support that facility.*

Chapter 21

I had gone to bed satisfied that I had reached out to Elena, that I had taken Jennifer's advice – the ball was now in her court.

But in the waking hours, that state of half consciousness where any disharmonies are brought vividly to life in their most negative aspects, I was worried. Had I worded it well? Had I said enough? Had I said too much? My only consolation was that there was nothing I could do about it now, the message was sent and however I worded it I would probably be having the same fears.

I had to wait it out. And wait it out I did as the day passed. She was certainly in no hurry to respond, or in a situation where she couldn't. Then as I was having my evening meal in the taverna my phone signalled a message. My heart was in danger of missing more than one beat as I looked at it with trepidation… It was Elena!

I feared opening it, even considering delaying its opening with the view that I would prolong my hopeful expectations but when I did, I was perplexed. The screen was virtually blanked out, much as parts of copied documents are where irrelevant text on that particular copy have been overtyped so they are not read. I didn't understand. Was it deliberate? Was it interference in the signal if she had maybe sent it from an aircraft at high altitude? Was that possible? What I did know was that I had no inclination of her response and that it would be difficult to construct another message.

And then, turning it over and over in my mind, when back in my room, yet another penny dropped. I'd asked her to reply with a kiss if she wanted similar messages and she had done just that – not one but a hundred and sixty eight of them. She had held her finger on the capital X key until it had run out of characters. They were virtually all joined up and filling the screen. I was elated! I had my answer! I cried again but this time it was with joy. Yes, I truly loved her and now I could believe in it.

I slept well and spent most of the morning trying to compose a follow up but I was spared the need with another message from Elena around lunchtime.

I love you too Matt. I love you more than I can find the words to express and I'm so sorry for what I said. What a silly, SILLY thing to say. I was frightened and I ran away but I'm going nowhere. Wherever I fly it's a dead end! I want to be with you and I'm coming home as soon as I can arrange it. XXX....

Again, she filled the remaining space with kisses. I wanted to tell everybody. I wanted to dance. I wanted to go up on the roof and shout! The world was now a more vibrant place, the colours, the sounds, the air itself. I walked out along the beach and I walked and walked until I reached that isolated cove where I first set eyes on her. But I didn't feel loneliness. There wouldn't be a lonely place on the planet now because wherever I was I would be filled with Elena's words. Loneliness became solitude once more and the silence again positively creative.

I sent her a brief message telling her not to be frightened, that we're in this together – her and me – and she replied.

Thanks Matt. Arriving Thessaloniki Sunday 1300 hours. I have old friends who have a retreat isolated in the mountains two hours north west of Thessaloniki and they have a room free for two nights and have offered it to us at a very special rate. If you could pick me up on arrival we could go straight there. What do you think???

I think that would be wonderful!!! I replied.

All confirmed. I've given my mother a list of a few things I'll need so she'll give you a bag to bring if that's okay. We'll get this sorted, Matt!! Can you handle a bit of Greek passion?

I can handle all the Greek passion in the world, if it's coming from you! Sunday 1300 hrs it is and I can't wait.

Sunday seemed to take an eternity to arrive but arrive it did and the drive to Thessaloniki was one of the most positive journeys in my life. I'd collected the bag from Maya and assuaged her fears. "Look after her, won't you!" she had said with emotion.

"We will look after each other," I told her but I saw uncertainty in her eyes.

"Hey!" I said, looking directly into her. "She loves you dearly, she loves this place and she loves her life here. I'm adding to that – not replacing it. We're coming back! Okay?"

She hugged me, putting her face to the side of mine and held my hand. "Thank you Matt," she said emotionally. "I have seen this coming," she added, as she continued to hold and squeeze my hand. "I'm pleased for both of you."

"Don't worry about a thing," I told her.

I was in very good time, I saw her plane land and endured an increased heartbeat as I waited for her to appear in the airport arrivals area. It seemed an eternity as I saw other passengers coming through having picked up their luggage and then as the last one came through there was quietness and my heartbeat quickened further. And I waited, fearful that something was not right but I realised that she would maybe have to 'debrief' or complete paperwork with the airline so I began to relax.

Then she appeared as if from nowhere – a solitary figure. In uniform, immaculate as always, towing her suitcase on wheels, a large shoulder bag and her jacket over her arm. She saw me and quickened her pace, half walking, half running in her heels. When she reached me in the open area, she put her bags down, her jacket over the handle of her trolley and we hugged each other such that observers would think we had been apart for a year or more. After some moments, we parted and looked into each other. We both had tears in our eyes and we smiled at each other with warmth and satisfaction.

"Let's get out of here!" said she. "Bloody airports!"

As I put her luggage in the car, she saw the bag that her mother had packed for her. "Thanks for bringing the bag Matt," she said.

"No problem but your mother asked me to tell you that she couldn't find your home rolled cigarettes or the condoms."

"Mm… of course she did!" said Elena, then she burst out laughing. "Right! My mother knows exactly where to find my home rolled cigarettes and I'm sure they're in the bag. As for the condoms, there aren't any. They're not necessary when you're on the pill, unless you are sleeping around, which I have never done." She put her finger on my nose and pressed it. "Okay?"

"Okay," I told her and helped her into the car. And as she manoeuvred herself, her pony tail swayed heavily from side to side and she stretched that uniform to its limits – elegant but inadvertently provocative.

Elena put the co-ordinates in the satnav and off we went. We drove through the outskirts of Thessaloniki and hit the open road towards the mountainous region that is North West Greece. She was leaning towards me with endearment, albeit restrained by her seat belt, occasionally touching my arm or shoulder as we talked. When I saw a layby ahead, I pulled in, cut the engine and we undid our seatbelts. We leaned to each other and we kissed, such that the public area of the airport wouldn't allow. I was aroused – I needed to touch her. I put my hand on her thigh and in the circumstances it felt erotic and as I squeezed, her skirt moved up and down her leg, the satin lining sliding effortlessly on her nylons.

I took my hand away. "Sorry," I said, but she got hold of it and promptly put it back on her thigh.

"I'm pleased to see that you are not going to stop me in my tracks again," I whispered.

"I will never hurt you again, Matt. I promise you." But we should be aware of being in a public place here. You know, English lawyer fondles air hostess in public. The press would have a field day."

"I thought the Greeks were more relaxed about such things."

"Mm, I wouldn't want to test that! Besides," she added, "I am in uniform. The airline would throw the book at you," said she with a cheeky chuckle.

"Would that be a text book or a novel?"

"The rule book!"

"Ah." We laughed, our foreheads together, before resuming our journey. Elena put her hand on *my* thigh and kept it there, giving me a little squeeze occasionally as we journeyed. The closeness between us had intensified, signalling the start of a new chapter – that of togetherness.

We stopped after about an hour at a roadside taverna for a coffee. "You must be tired having just come off duty?" I asked her.

"No I'm fine. I wasn't on duty on the way back. I hitched a lift to come back early. I had a pressing engagement back in Greece," she explained with a wry smile. Some lawyer from the UK, apparently, so she cut her official tour of duty short. "I've had quite a bit of rest. I'm in uniform just to make it official."

"Well you certainly look official to me," I told her, "and by the looks you're getting from others in this taverna, including the women, certainly to them as well. So official in fact, I'm having to wrestle with my impulses to hold myself in check. You will notice I have one hand holding the other down." She looked at my hands and then back to my face, restraining a laugh. "You do in fact look bloody fantastic!" I added.

Elena put a face to mine. "Did you say bloody fantastic?"

"Yes. As a scholar of Latin and the English language, that's the Anglo Saxon in me coming to the fore."

"So for all your studies, you find ancient Saxon the more fitting language to describe me?"

"At this very moment – yes"

"Good. I'll take that!"

We laughed together, so demonstrably that Elena's looks weren't the only reason for us drawing attention. "I will be careful not to touch you again while you are in an official mode," I said.

"I'm glad you understand the rules," I was told.

We resumed our journey with Elena telling me about her friends who own the retreat. Apparently they bought the buildings and the land and converted it themselves to establish the retreat. They did a deal with the airline for a joint publicity venture to launch it when they first opened and as the face of the airline she was in on the photo shoot. "A joint brochure was produced featuring both the airline and the retreat." she told me.

"And you were in that brochure – again in uniform?"

"Yes." She gave me an old fashioned look. "What are you thinking now Matt Rochester?"

"I'm thinking there was surely another poster there."

"Such as?"

"Such as... Mm... Rather than on a mountain top you'd be in front of the retreat. You would of course be in uniform and the caption would read...

MY NAME IS ELENA WITH ME YOU CAN SLEEP
AND YOU'LL FIND THE PRICES NOT TOO STEEP
I continued. "Another one for the director's private collection!
The retreat was fully booked for two years, the airline doubled
its number of flights into Greece, you got executive status from
thereon and you've been friends with the owners ever since,
getting concessions on rooms whenever you book."

"Stop the car!"

I stopped the car. She leaned across and kissed me all over my
face. "Oh I do love you Matt Rochester. And I love your sense of
fun – not least, the ability to make a case for or against any
situation. Your loss by the English justice courts is my gain." It
was a good five minutes before we resumed.

The retreat was indeed isolated – basically high in the
mountains in the middle of nowhere. It was a collection of several
renovated old stone buildings, linked together with single story
predominantly glass structures. It looked lovely – enticing in its
tranquil, beautiful setting.

Our hosts welcomed us with open arms and greeted Elena as
an old friend. They were very Greek both in appearance and
manner and were charming. Inside, the reception was in one of
the glazed structures, in natural wood with exposed timbers on
the ceiling. It was ultra-modern, contrasting with the old stone of
the original buildings. With so much glass, there was little
distinction between the outside and inside with the mountains
seemingly cloaking us all around. The place was silent, utterly
silent and with a wonderful feint aroma of incense giving a
soothing almost spiritual atmosphere, conducive to its purpose as
a retreat.

We were shown to our room which was in one of the old
buildings. It was sizeable, luxuriously but simply furnished in
modern taste with pale colours, sculptures and large artworks.

"Wow," I said with a smile. "Wonderful."

"I hope you will be very relaxed," said Helene, our host, with
a reserved discerning smile which, combined with her classical
features and her bearing, informed that she would be the vision
behind the design of the place and ruthless in pursuit of its
outcome. There was a bottle of Champagne with two glasses on

a tray on a side table and fresh flowers, unusual, perhaps more of the type I would expect to see in the mountains around us.

We unpacked and I walked into the en-suite with my toilet bag and was shortly followed by Elena. But I couldn't believe my eyes. If she was attempting to wind me up, she couldn't have found a more provocative way. She had untied her hair and shaken it loose and was still in her uniform and heels but her skirt was removed, revealing tight upmarket translucent knickers and classy hold up nylons with a darker band at the top with the brand woven in. She was making for the white robes that were provided.

I was stunned. Wildest dreams couldn't present a more evocative scenario. Whether it was deliberate or circumstantial I couldn't say but whilst I felt instant arousal, I couldn't help making a play of it at that moment.

"Ah, service! Could I have a glass of champagne please?"

Elena turned to me looking perplexed but after a moment, she realised that this was to be a charade. "Of course! Would you like anything with it?"

"What are you offering?"

"Peanuts," was her reply with a wry smile that covered a stifled laugh.

"Is that all?"

"You are touching my bottom. You could get banned from this airline for that."

"Really? Well if I'm getting a ban for that, the punishment can't be any worse if I touched you more meaningfully, can it? Could I know what a bit of Greek really feels like? Would you mind?"

She stepped closer to me. "Be quick about it!" I was told.

I pulled her tightly to me and fondled her bottom such that my imagination was compelling me. After a few moments she put her hands behind and lifted mine away. "I'm afraid there will have to be an enquiry about this," I was told. "They will be informed that there is touching and then there is touching up and that you are guilty of the latter. They must also be advised that you were clearly fully aroused at the time."

"Not surprising is it!"

"The enquiry will be convened later but in the meantime I will fetch your drink." She turned on the spot to face the door but before she took a step, she turned her head along her shoulder to look me in the face and scrunched her lips to form and execute a smouldering symbolic kiss and then made for the door with an exaggerated provocative walk. I remained stunned.

I heard a champagne cork pop and within a moment or two, she was back in the en-suite, her perfectly manicured hands placing a glass of champagne on the counter. "Will there be anything else?" she asked.

"Shouldn't your hair be tied back for cabin service?"

"You touch me again and I can assure you, sir, that a hair in your drink will be the least of your worries."

"Do you always call your passengers sir?"

"Only as a put down!" She again mouthed me a kiss and walked out of the room, suppressing a laugh. Seconds later, she came back in with purpose. "I came in here to get a robe," said she emphatically but then a smile confirmed that she had enjoyed our little charade.

We showered and changed and looked forward to dinner in our new surroundings, and with a closeness that we always had but also with the anticipation that to follow, would be a profound intimacy, the consummation of our relationship.

Chapter 22

The dining room was similarly themed. A highish ceiling with walls in pale muted colours, large unusual artworks on the walls, some sculptures and large potted shrubs almost presenting as small trees were strategically placed. The large windows had louvres to filter the light and each table had a lamp with a heavy silk shade, adding to the restful ambience. I counted fifteen occupied tables, mostly couples but the room was so spacious each of us had very much our own space.

"Penny for your thoughts," said Elena, endearingly.

"I was just contemplating the atmosphere in this room – obviously the creative genius of Helene – and how privileged I feel to be experiencing it with you sitting at my table. You compliment the ambience as a perfectly formed living work of art."

Elena held my hand on the table with both of hers and she looked into me with eyes as I've not seen them before. Very large, dark brown and made up as they always were but here, her pupils were enlarged, markedly so and her look was intense and I knew what they were saying and I was humbled.

"I'm so glad we came here, Matt. I think it is so right for us at this moment – two days to get things sorted. But I heard you've been a naughty boy," said she, in a matter of fact way.

"What?"

"That you irreverently touched an airline employee in uniform."

"Who told you that?"

"Grapevine! I hear they're considering sanctions against you." It would seem that Elena would enjoy continuing our little charade but now taking the role of a third party, not as a participant.

"Look! I was seduced by a drug induced, half undressed trolley dolly, wearing high heels and classy underwear. She was goading me."

"And you fell for it?"

"Well… yes, her looks, her figure…"

"And the uniform!" she interrupted,

"Half of it."

"Would that be the half that she was wearing or the half that she wasn't?"

"The combination of both," I told her. "Look I'm really very restrained – it's been so long. It… it just blew my mind."

"Mm… Bottlenecks can be nasty things, particularly with such provocation. Look, I'll do what I can – see if I can get the sentence mitigated to something less than an outright ban," said she, stifling a laugh while continuing to hold my hands.

"You deliberately wound me up, didn't you!!"

"I love winding you up, Matt Rochester! And I love sitting here with you at this moment. And… I'm looking forward to the rest of the evening. Okay?" she added, continuing to hold my hand and stroking my arm with her free hand, putting tingles through me.

And the rest of the evening was worth looking forward to. The meal finished, we moved outside for our coffee, but no brandy because we still had some of the champagne in our room. We sat under a parasol in the lee of the building. It was a warm night but there was a chill in the breeze from the mountain air.

Elena lit one of her home rolled cigarettes. Rolled in black paper, it was slightly thicker, shorter and more loosely packed than her usual brand and there was no filter. The smell was at once different, as having taken a small puff herself, she offered it to my mouth. "Gently," she whispered as we sat just inches apart, our eyes narrowing into each other giving the feeling that we were sharing something very special, if not covert.

"Wow," I whispered. "You're looking even more beautiful, even more desirable by the second. How can that be even possible in your case?"

Once in our room Elena adjusted the blinds, dimmed the lights giving a subdued moody light and rolled back the bed covers which in itself was suggestive. She then poured us some champagne and facing each other, we touched glasses.

"To us," she said.

"To us," I responded, "to our togetherness."

"So," she said, "I have spoken in your defence and in the circumstances and mindful of your honesty throughout this matter they have agreed to be more lenient than might otherwise have been the case." She then came close to me and in a purposeful, sombre whisper, said, "You are sentenced to spend the night in bed with this so-called trolley dolly and if you are still alive in the morning, have a nice day! Sentence to be carried out forthwith," she added as she unbuttoned my shirt and removed it. She then ran her hands sensitively over my chest before removing her dress,

She was stunning. I'd seen her in a bikini before and amazing as that was, it did nothing to prepare me for what I now saw. Her beautifully sculptured body contoured in tight fitting up-market underwear, in the moody lighting of our room, together with her classic features and long flowing hair, took my breath away. She loosened my belt and gestured for me to remove my trousers and underwear so that I stood before her compromised, my body with arousal there to be seen. "Mm. Hotshot lawyer morphs into rugged surfer with brains," she whispered in her deep tones. Then she slowly removed her bra and panties and we faced each other as never before. I was heady to the point where everything felt surreal and my knees weak. I wanted to touch her but I felt almost that I should ask permission, seeing a privilege, not an opportunity.

She stepped to me, put one hand to the back of my neck and the other behind my back and pulled us just lightly together as she tucked her head into the side of mine. I responded by putting my arms around her with a hand on that iconic bottom of hers. Her presence melted into me – her hair caressed my head and shoulders, which in itself was mesmerising and that extraordinary subtle musty perfume of hers, like something coming from the distant past, kissed my senses, adding drama and mystique. And I could feel the contours of her body lightly pressing into me – Elena as I have never seen or felt her before. I was ecstatic, otherworldly, shivering slightly but not from cold – my body was moving into a much heightened state. She looked into my eyes from point blank range, put her hand to my head and ran her fingers through my hair, taking it back along its length. "Okay?" she asked in that deep evocative whisper.

She got her answer by way of a kiss. A kiss that spoke more than words – soft, expressive and deeply meaningful, coming from deep within and it lingered. I sensed the slightest of tremors from her now and compelled to move on, we walked hand in hand to the bed. Compulsion was taking over and the inevitable would follow.

We laid together, kissing, touching, stroking as we rolled, each on top of the other, exploiting our feelings and the nudity itself, where in privacy, the very personal is shared – the unthinkable embraced.

We both had extreme arousal but despite prolonged abstinence on the part of us both, it was not hurried. It was calm and measured, artistic and deeply meaningful. It was as the slow movement to in an emotive symphony – expressive, not animalistic. We played each other like fine musical instruments, creating something so beautiful – a glorious mix of sex and love weaving together a tapestry so complex it was beyond reason. It was there for our emotions to construe and they did so with a free hand. Our subconscious came under its own law, our movements now involuntary and building.

I wanted her body, her physicality, her femininity. But more, I wanted her core, her essence, the woman herself and I penetrated deeply, exploiting feelings and sensations that were new to me. Still aware of her body, her hair, still entranced by that ancient scent but in deeper realms now and my senses were overwhelmed. Where was I? I was entwined with the very essence of another being and floating. It was surely ethereal and not of this world. God I loved her! And as the sensations built within me I saw a culmination ahead, the crescendo of this symphony, the reaching of which would be a portal to the unknown and it was almost frightening. Elena cried out as she pressed her head to the side of mine and hugged me tightly as she convulsed. And as I passed through, I'll swear I left this world, my final release giving sensations of an intensity not known to me previously. We were on this journey together and as we came out the other side the sheer bliss was ours to share.

And share it we did with few words necessary. Even over breakfast the following morning few words were forthcoming, we simply basked in a continued bliss. It was sombre, we were almost in reverence at what had happened but Elena did lighten things by confirming that I was still alive and that we should now have a nice day.

In consultation with Helene, she had planned a walk through the forest to a small mountain lake – a tarn – with a waterfall where we could swim if we wanted.

We set off with just a few things in a back-pack for the mile or so trek. Life couldn't be the same after last night and particularly so soon afterwards. Elena wanted to stay close and with contact, holding my arm with two hands or with one arm round me. Togetherness – we needed each other and we were seeing the world as one.

Our senses were heightened and the forest seemed like a Garden of Eden, the sounds, the colours – such vibrancy. Our state of being had created a calmness and awareness – a greater interaction with all about us. And it continued when we reached the tarn, a small body of water with a waterfall some fifty metres away at the far end. The green of the forest contrasting with the bare stone of the mountainside from which the water fell was toned with crystal clear water and deep blue sky. The sound of the waterfall was amplified in the silence and the place gave a feeling of solitude as if it was disconnected from known reality.

We didn't hesitate. We took off all our clothes, waded in to waist depth and then swam gently side by side towards the waterfall. To wear costumes was unnecessary with absolutely no-one about and to do so would have seemed at odds with the pristine water – it simply spoke naturalness. The water felt cold but we soon acclimatised and it was refreshing.

We still spoke few words. They weren't necessary. It was if we were in another dimension, a timeless dimension where everything was of the moment and where our thoughts communed. We found ourselves smiling at each other occasionally, appreciating what we were experiencing with one mind. As we neared, the sunlight interacted with a fine spray from the waterfall, dancing on the water, creating a visible florescence. We turned over and simply floated lifeless, basking in what seemed to be a magical realm. If last night had been the consummation of our relationship then this was surely the baptism. After a while we began a slow gentle backstroke, the sound of the waterfall gradually fading as we neared the shore

166

"Wow!" was one of the few words spoken as we walked back up to the grass and it wasn't misplaced. Being of one mind I could have said the same but Elena had spoken for both of us. We stretched our towels out on the grass, laid down on them and as Elena laid on top of me she pulled the second one over her, so we were intimately together but with some warmth after the chilly swim.

"So, do you think we have cleared some bottlenecks?" said Elena, bringing us back to recent events, "Or do we still have to bring in a psychiatrist." she asked, propping herself up on her elbows, her chin in her hands, her face just inches from mine.

"Right now I'm not sure of much at all. I'm in a void."

"Mm, me too, but that's good. You are certainly very relaxed. I see no tension. But," she continued, "we can't take any chances. We must work through a program to ensure there are no lurkers in there," she added, putting a finger to my head.

"A program?"

"Yes. We'll identify a series of scenarios and work through them. As I see it there is sex and there is making love. Making love is a joining of the souls, whereas sex is for clearing and preventing bottlenecks."

"How fortunate I am to have a daughter of Zeus at my side to point out the difference. You're certainly not wasted as a muse."

"Exactly! Now we'll start with the uniform thing once we get back."

"That could be a bit drastic – bordering on depravity."

"Bring it on. Those sort of fantasies aren't exclusive to men, you know."

"Is that right, Elena Costopolou?"

"Absolutely!"

"That sort of thing can play havoc with uniforms. What would the airline have to say about that?"

"I would simply tell them that I am capable of clearing bottlenecks and if they want customer service at the level to which they aspire, they must cost the price of a few uniforms into the fare structure. I could have the training manuals amended."

"Mm. If your imagination is given free rein, you might have to go on a course of sedatives."

"Did you know you've got an erection?"

167

"Surprising what a warm body and erotic talk can do, isn't it? Even after the numbing effect of a cold swim."

"Isn't it! Are you okay there?" she asked with concern but a cheeky smile.

"I'm fine," I told her. This is a strange one – a mix of cold water and erotic talk. I don't think my body fully understands it and may well have come up with the wrong answer."

She laughed and laughed. "I love you so much Matt," she said, her forehead touching mine. "Shall we get dressed and walk back? I've got a surprise lunch in mind for us."

The surprise was a further drive north from the retreat, to a small isolated village deep in the northern mountains. When the satnav announced our arrival we were in what was the village square. Houses surrounded us, some of them functioning as shops, with evidence of a trade being carried on. They looked hundreds of years old and the worse for time. The one that Elena walked us to had a few primitive iron tables and chairs outside and was functioning as a taverna. There were no roads as such and no terraces, our table and chairs sat directly on sun-baked earth. Few people were in evidence and those that were, were unhurried.

"Laid back or half dead?" I asked Elena.

"A good observation Matt," she said. "These ancient villages high up in the mountains, get by and even that with difficulty. Many of the inhabitants have moved away."

A man came towards us and spoke in Greek – he spoke no English. Elena chatted with him and explained to me that they were offering bread and cheese with pickles. There was no menu. "That sounds fine to me," I told her and she confirmed it with the proprietor.

"Will I be alright?" I asked.

"You will be surprised," I was told.

And I was! After a short wait a tray was brought to us bearing a basket of wholemeal crusty bread, a board of several cheeses and some pots containing pickles and relishes and one with olives. He put two wine glasses in front of us, pulled out a stopper from a half used bottle of wine and poured us some each.

"Tuck in," said Elena. It was all homemade she told me. The bread was crusty and tasty, and the pickles pungent, some sweet, some tart and the olives full sized and succulent. There was one relish, bright green in colour that Elena told me was from a berry that grew in the mountains nearby. There was goat's cheese, feta and a cream cheese and the wine was very palatable.

"They do all this themselves?" I asked.

"Yes. If you walked inside, you would be overwhelmed by the aromas. The bread oven, the relishes simmering on the range – it is their life."

"Where is their trade?"

"Neighbouring settlements, tourists like us, they get by but with difficulty, I'm sure."

"So how did you know of this place? You've obviously been here before."

"Yes. Remember the retreat promotional poster you spoke of – my name is Elena with me you can sleep. Well this particular guy wanted a guided tour and we found this place. He was of course a virtual stranger so I had to use a condom – or two!"

"And no doubt a home rolled cigarette?"

"Or two!"

"Well, all I can say is that on that occasion I'm so pleased your mother managed to find the condoms!"

She laughed her head off. "Oh I love winding you up, Matt."

"I've noticed."

"I can't wait to read your book. Still no title?"

"No but it will come."

After an unhurried and satisfying lunch I signalled for the bill and the man appeared and wrote on his pad, tore of the slip and put it on the table. All that was on it was E12. I showed it to Elena and she said, "Yes, twelve euros."

"What? I can't even get a cheese sandwich for that in London, even without a drink and we've both had wine."

Elena smiled. "This is a long way from London, Matt."

I gave him twice what he asked for and he looked shocked and wanted to give me some back but I shook my head and put my hand up. He looked humbled, folded up the money and walked inside to his wife. Moments late she came out and put a little bowl of what looked like small marzipan balls on the table. Then she crossed herself and she spoke in Greek.

169

"She says "God bless you. You are a kind man," Elena translated.

"Tell her that was wonderful and I'm very appreciative," I asked Elena and when she had translated, I held my hand towards the lady, which she took with both hers and nodded two or three times before returning to her house.

I felt emotional. I couldn't speak for a moment or two. "I'm sorry," I said. "I'm still emotionally raw after last night and with the swim and now this. I'm over-sensitive. It's found its way into me too easily."

"It's found its way into you because that is who you are at this moment and that is very beautiful," said Elena. "And may that continue because as I see you now, you have achieved what you came to Greece for. What you wanted to replace your life as a barrister and it may only now be apparent to you."

I looked at Elena and she was looking into me and with a depth that demanded understanding. And I had made love with her and what I was seeing now was what I felt in our moment of intimacy. It was beyond the physical, beyond the surface beauty and that is why it was like nothing I had ever experienced before and has laid me bare.

"The last twenty four hours have been cathartic for me. Thank you so much," I told her. "And here… here I have found a place where my words are irrelevant. I don't have to speak – just listen and it speaks to me. It creates a greater awareness. Another remote cove but with interaction of a different sort."

"And it's a place that's better for your presence being here, Matt and in more ways than one." She put her had on mine on the table and rubbed it lightly and with a smile said, "Shall we go?"

Yes a truly remarkable twenty four hours – I was a changed person. But I was not to know that an ill wind was again stirring, the wisps of which would manifest during the next twenty four hours.

Chapter 23

We were preparing to vacate our room when my telephone rang. It was Jennifer.

"Hello Jennifer," I answered.

"Hello Matt." She sounded uneasy, her voice breaking. "Matt, I'm really sorry to trouble you but they're holding Stefan for murder and I don't know what to do." She sounded almost out of her mind with stress.

"Murder?"

Elena, just hearing that word alone even before knowing the details, broke down immediately, putting her head in her hands and crying out "No! No!" She reacted immediately to the knowledge that I was again being involved.

"Who has been murdered Jennifer?"

"The private detective."

"He was still there? Why do they suspect Stefan?"

"His body was found at the bottom of a small cliff on his farm in a lay-by on the road. His neck was broken. They said he was seen with Stefan earlier the same day."

"Any other evidence? Witnesses?"

"Not that I know of but they're not saying too much"

"Has he been charged?"

"Not yet but the police say it is almost certain that he will be."

"Where is he being held?"

"At the police station. They've kept him there overnight. I don't know what to do Matt!"

I could hear the occasional stifled "No," from Elena as she continued to keep her head in her hands.

"Okay Jennifer. Listen! We're just about to leave this place. We're going to Thessaloniki to pick up Elena's car at the airport and then we will come straight back to the taverna. We should be there mid to late afternoon. In the meantime I'll make some enquiries. Try not to worry too much. I'll keep you posted on our arrival time and *you* let *me* know of any further developments."

"Thank you Matt. Thank you so much." Understandably, she sounded beside herself.

I rang off and gave Elena the details. "Jennifer has no right," she said. "She has no right, Matt! It's not fair!"

I cuddled her. "I'm not doing it for Jennifer, I'm doing it for Stefan. He's going to need all the help he can get."

"It's still not fair," she cupped my face in her hands and said, "All that we have achieved is going to be undone."

"You can't undo what's happened between us."

"I mean what we've achieved with your state of mind. You were in a beautiful place and now…" She cried.

I took her hands from my face and holding them, I looked into her and whispered, "Just stay close, okay?"

"Of course I will," she replied in reassuring tones. "I will stay very close."

"I thought deeply about possible scenarios before saying, "I must make a call."

"You have some thoughts?"

"I have a number of thoughts," I told her, "and I must try and check a few things out." I made the brief call.

"Cathy?" asked Elena.

"Yes, she'll ring me back."

And she did so as we were getting into the car. I asked Elena to excuse me as I walked a short distance away and took the call. I gave Cathy the scenario briefly and she agreed to make some enquiries and would inform me of her findings. She seemed pleased to have a little chat and to have an assignment.

Once back in the car, I got a sympathetic but prophetic look from Elena. "You and Cathy have a code when you speak," she said.

"Yes, we want to be absolutely sure who we're speaking to without relying on voice recognition. The nature of her work places her at risk at all times, so she is virtually anonymous and virtually unobtainable. It's more than a low profile, she is off the radar."

"Because her work is covert?"

"Much of her work is in grey areas, both for the security services and privately. She walks a thin line. For the government she works with a certain amount of impunity on highly classified assignments as you would expect but that would not extend to the private sector. I know the police use her from time to time and whilst they are not going to give their blessing for her to work in a certain way, they are very appreciative of the results, if you see what I mean. .Yes, she works in a world fraught with dangers. Loyalties can change in an instant, you are never sure who you can trust and whilst the rewards can be high, the dangers are real. Getting information legitimately for some people can be injurious to others, just as getting information covertly can make you a target. She works both sides of the line but is highly ethical. There is no direct line to her – the number you have is a dead end. She'll ring back if she wants to on an unregistered sim card."

"A burner phone?"

"Equivalent of. She has various sim cards and they change regularly."

We collected Elena's car and set off independently back to the taverna which was now very much my home. Some half way on the journey, I stopped to take a call from Cathy. We had a more detailed chat and she gave me some of her preliminary thoughts. She would need more time to investigate and would ring again as soon as she had more information if that was possible. I then telephoned Jennifer to ask her if she could arrange for the policeman on the case to meet us at the taverna late that afternoon.

"Are you okay?" asked a concerned Elena as we sat outside the taverna. I had told her of my telephone calls without going into detail and she asked me if I wanted to talk about it and when I shook my head, she continued to speak of everything but. She was there for me and as my mind worked, I was very grateful for her close presence.

I had a quick word with Jennifer when she appeared and then we all sat at an outside table to meet the policeman who had agreed to the meeting. It was the same one I had spoken with on the previous matter but this time, it was understandably more sombre.

"So," I asked him, "what is the latest position?"

"Stefanos remains in custody and will very likely be charged with murder," he said sombrely, looking at me directly.

"With what evidence?"

"The private detective's body was found by his farm, under a cliff at the side of the road. Stefanos was seen arguing with him earlier on his farm and as you are aware, they have history. Stefanos is a trained killer. Breaking a neck would be very simple for him – probably his preferred method."

"Could he not have fallen off the cliff?"

"No! That would have broken most if not all the bones in his body. This was a clean break to the neck with no other injuries."

"Stefanos is not a trained killer," I told him.

"He is a highly trained martial artist."

"A martial artist is trained primarily as a means of defence but more as a personal discipline – a discipline so profound and meaningful that the ability to kill is far less likely to be used than in the untrained. It is against their ethos. They could block, deflect, maim, or incapacitate with ease and the taking of a life would be anathema – against their very reason for being. And in the case of Stefanos, I can assure you that is the case. So whilst he may have the ability, the very discipline that would enable it, is the same discipline that would make him far less likely to use it than someone without that spiritual discipline."

"Your evidence is pure speculation." I leaned to him. "Can I ask you to consider postponing the question of charging for a short while? We are making further investigations and if charged, even if it is reversed, it creates a stigma that we would consider unnecessary and untoward."

"I will put forward your request but there are no guarantees."

"I say again, that your evidence is purely circumstantial."

"But with a high probability, Mr Rochester."

"At best, I can see a possibility not a probability and that is not enough to charge him. And if we are talking possibilities, virtually any local resident could be a suspect as could anyone passing through."

"But where would be the motive?"

"The fact that you aren't aware of a motive doesn't mean there isn't one. There could be any number of unseen possibilities with unseen motives."

"There is enough for a jury to consider."

"They would have no more evidence than you, so it would be purely character assessment which is totally unsatisfactory. Have you considered other possibilities?" I asked, turning my eyes to Jennifer and then back to him.

"If you are referring to Mrs Reeme's husband, we are well aware of certain jealousies and his connection to the deceased. We have looked into that possibility and he checks out!"

"I have early indications that he could be involved."

"Then your indications are misplaced. There is no record of Mr Reeme flying from London or arriving in Thessaloniki or Athens, to coincide with the event. Also the British police confirm that he has alibis for that period. So I'm afraid that one is as you would say – a dead duck. It's a non-starter!" he said profoundly.

"Perhaps we could meet again when our enquiries are complete," I asked.

"Of course," he said, giving me his card.

"Thank you." I stood up and shook his hand.

As he walked to his car, I looked at Jennifer. She looked drawn and uneasy but no words came. Elena took my arm, looked into me and said," Let's go for a walk."

It was lunch time the following day that I got a call from Cathy. She had been working prodigiously and I wrote down the facts as she gave them to me. I telephoned the policeman to ask him to meet me as soon as possible. Both Jennifer and Elena were present at that outside table at their own request.

"Mr Rochester," he said, his hand extended. "You have suggested we speak urgently."

"I have evidence that Alexander Reeme is involved to the point of being a suspect," I told him.

"As I have told you, Mr Rochester, there is no evidence of him being here and he has alibis in the UK."

"He didn't fly from London, he flew from Manchester and not directly to Greece but to Istanbul. From there he chartered a private flight to Volos airport. Not too far from here is it?"

"You have evidence of this!"

"Yes!"

"Airports don't give out passenger information, so it would seem that you have acquired information illegally so that may well not be admissible anyway. Your source needs looking into. The police should know about their activities."

"Strange isn't it? You spend your time trying to prove Stefan's guilt, now you're trying to disprove or discount his innocence. You are more concerned with the way the information was obtained than the implications of it. I'm not sure how my source obtained the information but she does work for the police on occasions, including Interpol and I don't think they are too fussed about her methods."

I leaned to him and spoke with depth and precision. "Alexander Reeme didn't have time to get false documents. He needed to get here in a hurry, so the best he could do was to cover his tracks by travelling indirectly." I took out a piece of paper and spread it out in front of him and told him, "Here are the details, dates, times, flight numbers and also the car hire company that provided him with a car at Volos Airport for three days. His return to the UK was the same in reverse three days later. Having the details, you can have this checked officially very easily and that certainly would be admissible. I would add that we are pretty certain that the private detective was blackmailing Alexander Reeme. We haven't gone sufficiently far down that route to offer evidence but you can do that. He may even admit it when he's cornered and that could well be the motive.

"Oh, and the broken neck?" I turned to Jennifer, and asked, "Wasn't your husband in the parachute regiment?"

"Yes, it's a family tradition. He did a single term."

I turned back to the policeman. "Breaking someone's neck would be in the basic training," I told him.

He studied my information, took out his phone and made a call. Translating his Greek, Elena leaned to me and whispered, "He's telephoned the car hire company at Volos. It would seem he knows the owner. He's asking him about the details you've given him." After a short pause, she squeezed my arm and whispered, "Mm, it seems it checks out!"

He looked straight into me for a while before saying, "The car hire is sufficient on its own to put Alexander Reeme here at the time of the murder and we'll quite quickly have the rest of this checked," he said pointing at the paper I had given to him. "I would think we will be very shortly asking the British police to make an arrest."

"They should also look into two counts of people bearing false witness – possible perjury."

He closed his eyes and nodded. "And I will of course authorise the immediate release of Stefanos."

"In the circumstances, we would want absolute clarity that Stefanos is no longer a suspect and is released unconditionally, by way of press releases in all of the local papers. And we would want that with the same prominence that was given to his apprehension – not just a single line insertion. That way we may be satisfied that his reputation and his standing in the local community is in no way compromised. We may then consider that no action on our part is necessary to clear his name," I said looking directly into him.

"I can arrange that," he assured. "I... I'm pleased that Stefanos is not involved."

"But you say you would most likely have charged him, without the evidence you now have. That is most unsatisfactory. A jury would have considered circumstantial evidence as debated by two lawyers and assessed his character as they see it. So the outcome would be dependent upon the skill of the lawyers and the juror's character assessment, which could be based on their own prejudices. He would have been found guilty or innocent with no certainty of the truth. Not only is it a travesty if an innocent person is found guilty – in this case of murder – but it would mean that the real culprit is still at large.

"You had no strong evidence against Stefanos and that is borne out by your making enquiries about Alexander Reeme. If you'd had stronger evidence against Stefanos, you wouldn't have broadened your enquiries but when you found that Reeme couldn't be involved, by your investigation that is, you came straight back to considering charges against Stefanos. That suggests to me that your priority was to obtain a prosecution rather than to establish the truth.

"Thank heavens there is someone out there who is capable of carrying out a proper investigation even if it may involve underhand methods," I told him.

177

He continued to look into me, his mouth slightly open but words wouldn't form. I stood up, took his hand briefly and walked away to the other side of the taverna. I wanted a change of thought. I wanted a change of focus. I breathed deeply and filled my lungs with the freshness of the sea air, I wanted the floral tinged scents of the local atmosphere, I wanted to fill myself with the new beauty and tranquillity that I had found. I wanted to breath it all in so that I was consumed by it all to the exclusion of all else.

Elena came running over to me. "Matt! Matt!" she cried and she put her arms around me, hugging me and tucking her head against mine. Her presence and her warmth added to the natural elements I was absorbing and it was calming.

"I've gone up through the gears and it's ratcheted me back to where I don't want to be."

"I know it has." Then still hugging me, she looked me straight in the face just inches away. She then ran a hand through my hair and grasped a bunch of it as she said in a broken voice, almost crying. "No! No! You're not leaving are you! Look, we'll have dinner together tonight. I'll reserve our favourite table in the corner and we can talk and talk and talk. And we'll spend the night together. Okay?"

Elena's eyes turned to Jennifer who had walked towards us and stopped, keeping her distance. I stood up and held my hand out and she came to us. "I'm so sorry Matt," she said, taking my hand, "I'm so sorry," she emphasised, then hugging me. Whether Elena had spoken to her or whether she had realised of her own volition, I wasn't to know but she obviously felt sorry for having involved me.

"Stefan has phoned me," she said. "He is being released unconditionally and without charge. They are driving him home – that is where he wants to be. He sounds very weak and I think he just wants to be with his cats and his goats. They have told him that they will be informing the local press of the situation and that they will do all they can to avoid any stigma."

"In that respect, good. I'm sure we both feel satisfaction that Stefan is cleared but I'm sorry for the possible outcome," I told her. One could only imagine what was on her mind as she looked at me disarmed, with tears in her eyes. "I think your husband is going to need a very good lawyer," I told her. "Very, being the operative word. I'm pleased to have contributed thus far but I cannot get involved any further."

"Oh, I understand completely, Matt. She apologised again and then said, "I'm so grateful for what you have done. ALL you have done. As I see it you have almost certainly enabled a more just outcome than would otherwise have happened if the police had just blundered on and I insist on recompensing you and your source. There must have been a lot of time spent on this as well as costs incurred and I really insist on paying for it."

"I appreciate that Jennifer but I personally will not accept any payment for what I have done. Again, I acted as a friend. Regarding my source, yes I am aware of what was involved and I have made it clear to her that I will pay for her time and any costs."

"Well I will pay those. Her fee and her costs. I absolutely insist Matt, whatever it costs."

"Okay, Jennifer, thank you, I'll speak to her on that. So far as you and I are concerned we go forward as friends?"

"We continue as special friends, Matt, whatever ensues," she said with great sincerity. Her moist eyes took on a slightly different projection as she then said, "As a point of interest, my husband's family motto is, 'Suscipere et bene exsequi.'"

"Mm… Undertake and execute well," I translated. Jennifer's expression was now one of irony.

Chapter 24

We had our table in the corner. It was partly secluded by a large shrub and afforded some privacy. We'd not long sat down and were awaiting the food that Elena had laid on for us, when one of the local Greek regulars walked up and put a bottle of champagne on the table between us and keeping his hand on the bottle, he said something in Greek.

"Oh…! Oh," said Elena again. "He says…" then she spoke to the man as if to get clarification before translating for me. "He has spoken a very old Greek saying. It is difficult to translate exactly but what he is saying is, 'thank you for what you have done.'" She again clarified something with him and then continued, "He says you now have many friends here. Word has got round. Stefanos is loved here."

I bid Elena to thank him for me and to say I am honoured. I shook his hand and as he returned to his friends at a nearby table, Elena got up. "I'll be back," she said as she walked purposefully to the bar. She returned with a handful of champagne glasses which she put in a cluster on the locals table. Then she took the bottle of champagne from our table and beckoned me to join her as she popped the cork and while it was still fizzing, she made a deft single circular movement over the glasses pouring some in each. It was done with panache, symbolic of the gesture made by the locals and in itself signalled 'all friends together.' They each took a glass, sipped from it, murmuring in Greek and as Elena and I also took a sip, a bond of friendship was established.

"You're a hero," said Elena as we re-seated ourselves at our table. They will never forget. That is something else you get with Greek people – apart from the passion that is – gratitude and loyalty. They will *never* forget!" She put her hand on mine and squeezed it. "You're not going anywhere are you?" she added, her earlier thoughts still with her and causing concern.

"Look, I'm not going anywhere without you sweetheart. In fact I'm not going anywhere at all. I have something to tell you."

She looked at me and asked in a coy voice, "What? What is it you want to tell me?"

"I'm thinking of putting an offer in on a villa."

She was utterly astonished – aghast no less. She was speechless for a moment and then, breaking out in enthusiasm she asked, "Where?"

"Up the mountain road past Jennifer's," I told her nodding my head in that direction."

She thought for a moment before saying, "There's one up there still awaiting renovation but I understood it was sold some time ago."

"That's right but the fortunes of the guy who bought it have changed. He can no longer afford the project so he's looking to get his money back."

"Oh Matt! That could be a lovely villa. It's in a wonderful position."

"That's what I think. I had made enquiries but I didn't want to say anything until I was sure it was a possibility. The agent has just phoned me while I was in my room getting ready and I'm meeting him at the villa together with Jennifer's builder, the day after tomorrow to discuss options and possible cost. Would you like to come along?"

Elena was beside herself with enthusiasm. "Yes! Yes, I'd love to." Then she looked a little unsure. "They might not accept your offer."

"They might not but I'm prepared to pay the asking price if necessary, unless the builder finds something untoward."

Greek passion showed no restraint. I was set upon, bestowed with kisses as she leaned across the table, pulling me towards her, leaving me in no doubt that in her eyes I was doing the right thing. "Don't let today get to you Matt. We're in this together, you and me and we'll get through it. We can plan another trip away but perhaps longer this time. We can swim in the sea, maybe go to the retreat again – use it as a base. Then we could drive into the mountains again – find some remote villages. And I'd take a uniform with me. What do you think?"

"Why a uniform?"

"Therapy! Look we have agreed that we can't take the chance of any un-cleared bottlenecks and now there is the added need for you to have a release. Get rid of the tension that Jennifer has unfortunately clobbered you with. Bring you back down through the gears. All in all a bit of severe therapy wouldn't go amiss. Okay?"

"Okay. Wow! I think that sounds wonderful but what about your job?"

"That's okay. Look, before I got your text, I was working almost with tears in my eyes. People were asking me what was wrong. Word got through and I had a phone call from one of the directors. I told him I was now in a relationship and it needed some sorting. He insisted that I took paid leave for as long as it takes to get things settled. Then he said that they are not going to lose me and basically I can plan my own hours and shifts, airtime or training. And now of course I have to make sure you are okay Matt. I mean it, we're in this together."

She was lovely, she really was there for me – warm and supportive. "I love you so much," I told her.

"And I you, Matt," she replied. "Believe it!" Then she traced my nose with her finger saying, "I think you are amazing. Your reasoning, your dealing with the police *and* not least Jennifer. I felt privileged to be at your side. I sat in on a masterclass. It was very well done," she added. "You've proved Stefan's innocence."

"No, I haven't, any more than I have proved Jennifer's husband's guilt."

Elena looked at me deeply disturbed, her eyes showing a fear that there may still be an element of doubt.

"What I have done is to offer another greater possibility of guilt than the police have so far established with Stefanos."

"You still think there is a possibility that Stepfnos could have done it?"

"If you're taking council's opinion, I would suggest that Alexander Reeme is quite probably guilty."

"Probably? But he has lied with his alibis and taken the trouble to disguise his travel route and the car hire places him in the area."

"And with a motive if we are right with the blackmail aspect. But even with all the circumstances against him, a good lawyer would argue there is no direct evidence of him actually committing the murder. He could have come here with the intention of doing it but then found that it was done for him, possibly even for unconnected reasons. I could present various scenarios."

"No…! No Matt…"

"No," I interrupted. "I'm not getting involved. You heard me tell Jennifer that I can't and anyway, I think he would be better off with a current London lawyer. I don't want to be involved. I've done what I saw as necessary and I don't think Stefan will be troubled any further. I want to resume my new life."

Elena nodded. Then as a further thought, she said, "Cathy was amazing. How does she do it?"

"She is amazing and the answer to your question is, 'I don't know.' I think there is a principal involved similar to reverse engineering when scientists want to establish how something was or could be made. They imagine a finished product or how it would have to be to function and then take it apart in reverse, if you see what I mean. I think Cathy would establish how a situation would have to be for a given scenario and then unpick it from the end, not the beginning. Difficult to understand? Not for her! She would start by putting him in this area and if the two main airports didn't yield a result then she would try local airports. Hence Volos, then local car hire and then trace it back to the beginning."

"Clever."

"Very! But her being clever is off the scale if you remember, particularly around computers. How far her methods are off limits so to speak I don't know and that is the aspect I don't want to know. She has ethics and I trust her in that respect."

"We could invite her out here for a holiday – at the taverna. I'd love to meet her. Do you think she might like that?"

"I could put it to her."

"She could go surfing with Stefanos. They sound as they would make a great combination."

"I know what you mean but remember her persuasions are possibly different and anyway you wouldn't want to cause Jennifer to bristle."

"Oh yes! Maybe she might pair with Jennifer," said Elena, teasingly

"Look, if she did come here, it would be for a thank you holiday, not for possible matchmaking. If you upset the status quo, you could invoke jealousies and we don't want another murder on our hands."

She laughed. "Quite right," she uttered. What's Jennifer's husband like, Matt?"

"Very corporate, driven but charming. He is successful and it shows."

"Good looking?"

"Mm... attractive I'd say."

The evening didn't disappoint. It never did with Elena. From the profound to the frivolous, it was meaningful and fun with hardly a pause for breath let alone for food intake. From touching interaction with the locals with complimentary champagne, to talk of villas, of Cathy and her methods, of Jennifer's husband, to relationships and possible murder. Add in the cuisine which was selected by her and carefully explained to me as we consumed it, along with a few sampling dishes and no, it certainly didn't disappoint. It never did. And she looked stunning. She was so real and with our coffee and brandy outside under the old lantern it was absolutely amazing and that was before I spent the night with her, which wasn't previously on the cards.

Chapter 25

The day after tomorrow soon arrived when we would drive up to the villa to meet the agent and Jennifer's builder.

Seeing it afresh, it seemed so right and I was hoping that the builder wouldn't find problems. It was with several other villas in a cluster but they were very well spaced and all on different levels as the mountains dictated. We all shook hands and walked inside with Elena holding my arm with both her hands, signifying both her enthusiasm and her support.

The builder took himself on his own tour with just the occasional prompt from the agent. He took his time, pondering, assessing, and occasionally scraping or prising with an implement he was carrying. He took about half an hour before coming back to us with his sketch pad.

"You're thinking along the lines of a traditional renovation likes Jennifer's?" he asked

"Yes, very much so," I confirmed. "With natural stonework and your special aged rendering and with Stefanos doing the non-structural woodwork. I would consider a decent size pool and a large terrace over there," I pointed.

"Yes, it would fit," he said. His English was a little sparse but Elena interpreted where necessary. "I can't see any major problems" he said – "nothing we can't work round. I would quote in stages as we progress."

I asked Elena to ask him for a ball-park figure. He pondered at length, hand on chin. "Two hundred to two fifty thousand," he said, as he juggled his hands. "It also depends on the pool and terrace, depending on what you want. I can't quote you fully at this stage," he re-iterated "but I say to you Mr Rochester, I want the work very much. I will do a good job and I will save you money where I can. I love my work..." said Elena in translation.

"He is very good," said the agent.

I put my offer to the agent which I thought was reasonable and he telephoned the vendor there and then. The agent put his hand over the phone and told me that the vendor couldn't afford to sell at a loss but he would split the difference with me. I nodded and he confirmed it with the vendor.

"You've got yourself a villa," said the agent and I asked him to tell the builder that a deal was done. I then asked Elena to tell the builder he had himself a job and I looked forward to working with him. The builder was ecstatic. Work, other than small repair work was scarce in the area and he needed the job. We shook hands and he left the site a happy man. Almost as happy as Elena who was absolutely delighted to say the least as she ran into one of the rooms and did a little dance.

"Stefanos will love this," she said. "The split levels with the lower courtyard, the old characterful doors, the stone stairs outside winding up to this higher terrace and there are mature shrubs everywhere, climbing up the walls," she added as we climbed the steps.

"I'm sure he'll do as he did with Jennifer's – free the shrubs from the walls and pull them away for renovation and then put them back, preserving the character and atmosphere that would otherwise take years to re-establish."

"Do you think you might have a pool?" she asked.

"Yes, that flat area on the other side really lends itself to it and with another attractive terrace. It would be secluded and very private there."

"Mm, no costumes needed," said she, her eyes slightly crossed as she confronted me at very close range.

"So could you see yourself here?"

She swung round, walked out onto the terrace and mimicked a ballet dancer expressing a scenario. "Could I see myself here?" she asked. "I could see the Bougainvillea, the Oleander climbing over the balustrade here on a warm summer evening their perfumes combining with that Tamarisk tree to bathe this terrace in a heady scent. I could see you and I here together having a drink, just having had a swim in the pool below. I could hear the music faintly influencing the mood as we look out to the mountains. Add the cuisine, the conversation and the couture to the equation, not to mention my breasts and the whole thing is a no-brainer. Would I be invited, do you think?"

"For lunch?" I said, teasing her.

"I was thinking maybe more. Remember I do bottleneck clearance too."

"You haven't mentioned your bottom."

"I'll throw that in – part of the package."

"If I touch it would I hope to die?"

"You've touched it enough over the last few days and you are still alive. I suggest you keep on doing it! As you might say in your profession: 'Establish a precedent!'"

"Mm… Okay, you're invited. But only on one condition."

"What's that?"

I took her hands and pulled her close to me and looking directly into her I said, "Elena Costopolou, daughter of Zeus, muse extraordinaire, Greek cuisine aficionado to airline executive and two or three other Elenas in between. Love of my life! Will you marry me?"

Her expression was one I have not seen on her before, in fact I can't recall having seen it at all.

Eyes wide to the extent that they might pop out and her mouth open like a basking shark feeding on plankton. She studied me and looking into each eye in turn and digesting the depth of my expression, she cried out! "YES!" Then she shouted, "YES! YES! YES!" and she threw her arms around me and gripped me tightly as she cried. After a few moments, she let go, turned round and went further out on the terrace half running, half dancing. She stopped, turning to face me and hesitated for a moment just staring at me and then she ran to me and flung her arms around me again. "Yes! I'll marry you Matt. Of course I'll marry you! I'll tell you something. If you had asked me on that first day we walked into the village, I would have said yes. It was amazing. The conversation, the interaction, I've never experienced that before. I was blown away."

"Well I'll tell you something. In my mind I was wanting to ask you – for the same reasons. In those few hours my life was changed irrevocably. As you say, blown away."

"It was love at first sight."

"I thought… well maybe… if you agree of course and it would be your decision, we could get married in your little church in the village."

"Oh!" Would you do that?"

"Of course. I think that would be lovely – if they do weddings there, it's so small."

"Yes, they do. They can't get many inside obviously, so they leave the door open so the people outside are part of it. I would love that," she said, her eyes still filled with tears. "We could have the reception at the taverna."

"Sounds wonderful," I told her.

"Can I tell my mother?"

"Of course you can! You can tell the world!"

"I won't tell anyone else until we get the ring."

"Which will be very soon, sweetheart. We'll go in to Thessaloniki or Athens and sooner rather than later. My feeling is that you will be less likely to see our relationship as with 'non attachment' if you have my ring on your finger."

"Oh Matt! I'm so happy. I've got myself a rugged surfer with brains and I'm going to love you to bits forever."

"That's not enough. I want it forever and a day!"

"You've got it!" she said with feeling. "I must give some thought to my job. As I've said, the airline will fit in with me, which is good. We'll work out together what suits us. I wouldn't want to give it up completely at the moment but be assured that if I did, I would keep a uniform or two. You know, for therapy."

"But that wouldn't work."

"Why?"

"It wouldn't be authentic. It would be just a prop. A piece of kit for re-enactment – playacting! It's got to be for real to have meaning."

"I see what you mean. The psychology is wrong. I must be going on or coming off duty. So basically I've got to keep my job on until you can't rise to the occasion anymore, which as I know you now, that could be forever and a day too."

The conversation was nonstop as usual and again going from the profound to the frivolous at the blink of an eye.

"Do you know, I've finally got the title for my book?"

"Really? Oh tell me Matt what is it? Tell me!"

"Well it's not a salient point in the story, it's more of a thread that runs through it."

"Tell me, tell me!"

"The Goat Herder."

If you enjoyed reading this book, your kind consideration to leaving a review on the Amazon website would be much appreciated.

James

Printed in Dunstable, United Kingdom

66627834R00111